Afterheat

Also by CD Collins:

Albums:
Kentucky Stories
Subtracting Down
Carousel Lounge
Clean Coal/Big Lie

Poetry:
Self-Portrait With Severed Head
(Ibbetson Street Press)

Short Stories:
Blue Land (Polyho Press)

Coming Soon to Empty City Press:
Everything Is Conditional Love Poems by Donavon Davidson
Kinesiophobia by Meghan Guidry
I, Dagger by Keith Backhaus

Afterheat

-*A novel*-

CD Collins

Empty City Press

EMPTY CITY PRESS

'Afterheat'
An Empty City Press Book

Published by:
Empty City Press
1109 Rayville Rd
Parkton MD 21120

All Rights Reserved. No part of this publication may be reproduced or transmitted in any form or by any means electronic or mechanical, including photocopy, recording, or any information storage and retrieval system now known or to be invented without permission in writing from the publisher, except by reviewers who wish to quote brief passages in connection with a review written for inclusion in a magazine, newspaper or broadcast or online media.

Excerpts of this Novel have appeared in the following publications:
StoryQuarterly—'Home Fires'
&
Salamander—'Heat'

Copyright © CD Collins 2015
Second Printing 2016
Book and Cover Design: Kerin Backhaus
Front Cover: "Body Lace" by Babette Meyers
Back Cover: "Fourth of July" by Diane Devlin

ISBN: 978-0-9802352-2-7

For Lula and Henry

Acknowledgments

Profound gratitude to my colleagues, mentors, friends, and family who supported me in the evolution of this work: Babette Meyers, Pamela Painter, Lexa Marshall, Jenny Barber, Carol Dine, Linda Cutting, Pam Bernard, Gary Miller, Bob Dall, Karen Roehr, Liz Buchanan, Holly Lecraw, Janet Hays Johnson, James Blandini, Allison Lund, Jutta Kausch, Avery Rimer, Dana Winchester, Stephen Collins, Danny Marcus, Susan Bernstein, Peter Brown, Leslie Shultz, and Martha Spizziri.

Table of Contents

1 Flash Photography 9
2 Vance 16
3 River of Heaven 21
4 Lalique 37
5 The Carousel Lounge 53
6 Heat 70
7 Hurricane 121
8 Big As Life 141
9 The Search for Wendy Starr 159
10 Home Fires 177
11 The Gold One 193
12 Laundromat Jesus 215
13 Free Enterprise 231
14 Nightfall 253
Epilogue 273

Chapter 1
Flash Photography

After the surrender of Japan, American servicemen bivouacked on Hiroshima ash to study the effects of the bomb and to assist with the wreckage. One of the soldiers, my father, Claytis Chambers, a teenaged boy from Vance, Kentucky, toured the destroyed sites with his company. Emperor Hirohito hosted the entourage, making sure the honored guests were well fed and tended in the bars and bathhouses of his country.

Years later, my father drove our Pontiac down the curving roads of rural Kentucky in the autumn afternoon. My mother, Pearl, rode alongside in the front seat. My brother, James, and I looked out the backseat windows, playing our favorite car game: naming everything we saw "Grass, grass, tree, road,

Afterheat

road, road, car! Grass, grass, cow!"

"That's enough," Mom called to the backseat without turning her head.

James and I shot sly glances at each other and mouthed the words. "Grass, grass, road, road." We were headed for Sky Bridge, where Dad planned to try out the new movie camera he'd bought Mom for her birthday. The camera lay between them on the warmed vinyl of the front seat. The car was painted a rich bronze and sported a replica of an Indian head as a hood ornament. Mom once said that whenever Dad came home drinking, his eyes were as bloodshot as that Indian.

My father was a handsome man with dark, wavy hair and heartbreaking blue eyes. During the week, both my parents worked government jobs, but on weekends Dad built and remodeled houses with his brother. Though a small man, my father could balance a flat of bricks on one arm while hoisting himself up a ladder.

Straddling the hump in the floor well, I poked my head over the seat to ask Dad what they ate for supper in the army. I liked hearing about food when I was hungry, like right now. My foot was on James' side, so he tapped my shoe, a warning.

"Well, let's see." Dad stroked his smooth jaw with his fingertips. "Hardtack bread, maybe a can of spaghetti and meatballs as the main course, a chocolate bar and a pack with four cigarettes. Those were the C-Rations." He always named a different main course. Tuna and noodles, cheese discs, cookie sandwiches. I wanted to taste them. I thought of C-Rations as Sea-Rations, the kind of food you ate when you traveled overseas.

Satisfied, I nestled back in my seat and surveyed ramshackle houses with rusting trucks in the front yards. I collected Dad's tales about the war. We pitched tents on acres of ash, he said. Shadows froze onto the walls. Later, I would learn that the wall impressions were actually photographs of people as they dematerialized.

The hills were steeper now, and on the next rise, I spotted Sky Bridge, so high up I could picture myself walking on up to heaven. "Hi God," I'd say to him if he came out to meet us. "Got a bone to pick with you." Then we'd settle down on golden thrones and have a talk.

"Grass, grass, road, road," James whispered.

"Gravel, gravel, dog, dog!" I chanted.

"If you all are good, you can go to the movies

Afterheat

tomorrow," Dad called as he steered around a sharp curve, and we hushed up.

We loved the downtown theater. Our grandfather, Pa, worked there as a ticket taker and ran the concession stand. He let James and me in free and gave us one popcorn and one candy bar each, then we disappeared to opposite sides of the theater.

I always picked the kind of candy that lasted longest, Sugar Daddies or Atomic Fireballs. I'd open them after the cartoon and try to make them last all the way through the movie, which was usually about monsters, like *Attack of the Giant Leech*. I pitied the movie monsters even if they scared me half to death. They were always too huge and ugly to make a good impression on the beautiful women they loved.

That afternoon, we hiked all the way up to the sandstone formation that connected two low mountains. While I traced a forefinger in the names carved into the top of the bridge, my father filmed the high ridges and foothills of the Appalachian countryside. The whole panorama looked to me like mounds of Trix cereal, the kind the silly rabbit could never eat even though it was his goal in life.

Neither of my parents realized then that when

they would watch those movies thirty years later, the landscapes would not interest them. Perhaps if they had moved from home, the once familiar hillsides would have comforted them, or, if like the mountains to the east, which had been blasted apart for coal, they would have been pleased to have captured some remnant. But the mountains around Vance remained constant, accessible to them on any Saturday drive.

Did my father think my mother would always have that same determined female strut? Did he think the upturned faces of his children would forever remain within his sight? No, he had not lingered long enough, had caught only a few frames: one of James, straightening his back, trying to be the little man in his baggy corduroys, a snippet of me pulling up my underwear after peeing in the woods, a shot of Mom's mischievous expression, her hand waving as he panned past her while focusing on the horizon.

No one could ever quite see my face in home movies, just a blur as I turned my head, as though I believed that being in sight of the camera's eye was somehow hazardous. My father was a careful photographer with a steady hand. He kept rolls and rolls of film in metal canisters in the top of the closet, collecting proof: the flaming hills; our dog, a

Afterheat

German Shepherd jumping the fence again and again; the shimmering rainbow hovering in the mist at the bottom of Broke Leg Falls.

There were many things that afternoon that my father could not fathom. Lifting me over the rock fence on the way down the mountain, he felt no symptoms of what was to come: the gouty arthritis, the odd erosion of enamel that melted his teeth down to their roots, all those things that would befall him and the servicemen who served alongside him. He could not have predicted our accident.

As he zipped the camera inside its case that afternoon, he was thinking of the future unrolling before him like the roads beneath his powerful car, of the house he would build for his family, with crystal faucets and gold-glazed sinks. They would walk on plush carpet two inches thick and drink highballs beside their swimming pool. His children would go to college. They would hold their heads up high. He could picture all this as clearly as the brilliant sky through the windshield of his Pontiac. All he had to do was focus on the road ahead and step on the pedal.

My father told me that when the bomb exploded over Hiroshima, the crew on the plane noticed a taste like a dissolving lozenge of lead, the taste of nuclear fission. I liked the sensation of something dissolving in my mouth, the buttery brown sugar of suckers, the layers of Atomic Fireballs. Swallowing, I watched the sad monsters trying to please the women with blond hair like my mother's. But the beasts only succeeded in frightening them or killing them by accident. That Sunday, I marveled at the tiny Japanese fairies singing for their mother. I absorbed those movies in the cavernous theater into my senses as I did my parents' arguments, my father's long silences. I was aware of how crowds parted to let them pass in their stylish clothes, how their hair shone as I gazed at them from the back seat of the car. I studied them carefully and listened when they didn't know I was listening. It all came to rest deep in my cells, forming and transforming them. I learned without knowing what I learned, or even that I learned. I knew without the words of knowing.

  I took each fireball out of my mouth as I sucked it, examining each layer, the red coating, the thick pink layer underneath, then halfway through, the hard crunchy shell. I resisted the temptation to crack it with my back teeth and allowed it to melt slowly. I gazed up at the images, swallowing, hotter and hotter, the white, stinging cinnamon, the burning at the core.

Afterheat

Chapter 2
Vance

In my hometown, your name unfolded like an accordion book, revealing your entire history. You were born into a caste, a genealogical blueprint of expectation as plain as the facts on your birth certificate. It was hard not to take what you were handed. Fairchild meant doors flew open all the way to an Ivy League school; Taulbe meant doors whisked shut in your face if you dared set foot on the threshold. The black folks lived on a rocky hill in the East End, while the West End was reserved for brick mansions with wide sloping lawns. If you were a Goldiron, you mowed those lawns and tended the rambling flowerbeds. A Goldiron meant sparklers and Fritos on Friday night because that's all the fun you could afford and that the roof over your head was rented.

CD Collins

Inside the mansions lived families whose very mention stirred a fragrant breeze, names that conjured images of croquet games played by children dressed in white linen, and of wintering in the Caribbean. These were the Fairchilds, the Graysons, the Downs—handsome families whose gestures were calm and elegant because they did not have to grab to get what they wanted, and soft, well-modulated voices because they did not have to raise them in order to be heard.

In our town, your name determined if you were placed in calculus or general math. It decided your salary, who you married and where you were buried. The part of town you were born in was a taproot that extended down into the earth, anchoring you for better or worse.

If you were a Chambers, it meant you had dirt under your fingernails and skin stained from whatever crop you were handling—rust red when stripping tobacco in the fall, or indigo-palmed in summer when blackberries were in the full.

Our third-grade teacher, Mrs. Oldham, stood tall behind her oak desk calling out "Anderson... Bellamy...Bartley...Chambers..." and we called back "Present," waiting to hear the flunk-out who'd answer "President." We all lived in the same town—neighbors,

Afterheat

schoolmates, bankers' kids, kin—so, in elementary school, the roll call each year sounded nearly the same.

Mrs. Oldham was a willowy woman, who wore shirtwaist dresses with patterns of tiny fruit. When we answered, she riveted her eyes on us like a brand. She was deciphering the puzzle, reading backward into the past and forward into the future. "It's all in the blood," people said, as though it were impossible to pry apart the pieces of your destiny and put them back together some other way.

A few school kids lived downtown, not in one of those richly painted Victorians stationed like queens along Green Street, but where Green crossed over Broadway, dropped on down to Locust Street with its railroad tracks and strip of honky-tonks, the names spelled out in neon—The Blue Moon, The Walking Horse Inn, Ed's Rear-Back-and-Rock Hall of Dance. These were the Chapson family with their golden skin and spellbinding, sea-colored eyes, the lank-haired, big-shouldered Franks—kids who grew up tough and smoking, wearing tight T-shirts and cut-off jeans. They hammered out their lives against a hardscape of concrete, glass storefronts, and run-down brownstones.

Downtown was for shopping and rough

dealings after sundown, not a place you actually made your home. More than the rural kids, the downtown ones ran the risk of going wild. Every year a drunken carload of them would go airborne in a spot called Death Dip, their soaring vehicle ripping off tree branches fifteen feet in the air. Maybe they believed if they floored it fast enough and hard enough, they could actually escape this town. State troopers would find them in the fields the next morning, a leg here, arm there, their flesh torn all to pieces.

"Pure Locust Street," people said, whenever any of them went astray.

Kentucky is prone to acts of God, earthquakes, plagues of tornadoes, floods. So when they started having bomb drills at school, we thought of it as just more excitement. When the air horn blared, we hit the oak floorboards and scrambled under our desks as instructed. The Bomb was coming, the big red button pushed by the wooly-bully finger of a depraved Russian.

People talked on and on until finally our town got its bomb. It arrived in the form of an explosion that blew up just two families, the Bonaventures and the Chamberses. The newspaper ran photographs of the blaze that reared high above the giant oaks and

Afterheat
melted the tar road in both directions.

"A blast like an A-bomb," the caption read.

The story passed immediately into legend. Those with first-hand information enjoyed a brief celebrity.

"I felt the earth shake standing on my back porch out on Harper's Ridge."

"I was up at the hospital when they rolled them in. Little Chambers girl was the worst off, on account of her being so young."

Some speculated that this tragedy foretold that Vance would be spared. Others said it was an omen of worse misfortune to come. True or not, the details of the explosion were stored in the collective memory along with the tale of the baby Dalton girl with the milk allergy who died from a pat of butter, and the nine-year-old swim champion who drowned in Dr. Isaacs' well.

Chapter 3
River of Heaven

I was born a Chambers. Although my father came from dirt farmers, he'd stared bombs in the face and traveled too much of the whole wide world to let a little town like Vance tell him who he was. He deserved the good life because he'd fought the good war. He set his sights high. He wanted to see his dreams manifest, like God on Creation Day, and to do that he needed money. Everything was just going to get bigger and better. His first dream was to own a house for his family. 'You built your house or you died trying,' was the Chambers family philosophy.

We were English on the Chambers side, Scots on my mother's, the Tudor side. The Chambers clan lived out in the country, the Tudors downtown. My grandfather, Pa Tudor, had written a genealogy that

Afterheat

showed us descended in a straight line from Mary, Queen of Scots. If any jewels had been handed down, they'd been lost in the trail across the Appalachian Mountains, placed at intervals, maybe, so the young ones could follow, then grabbed up in the beaks of birds. Blue jays, I guess, who wanted sparkle in their nests.

Still, Tudor was a grand old name in Vance, known for its artists and charming men who married wealthy women and ran through their money. Pa had done that too, although after he lost his wife to sugar diabetes, he'd hung on to the house by renting out the upstairs and working in his retirement at the Trimble Theater. Tall and bespectacled, Pa outfitted himself like a senator in dark suit pants, a gleaming white shirt, and wide ties in soft, metallic shades. While our parents worked, he kept James and me from drowning in the storm drains or dropping headfirst from the jungle gym and smashing our heads on the concrete.

After James and I came thrashing and bawling into the world, Pa typed our names onto a slip of paper and pasted it in the back of the genealogy book. Later, he included a snapshot of James and me looking elfish in matching red wool sweaters. My brother was barely a year older than me; Irish twins we were called, though we weren't Irish. We weren't Catholic, either, so my parents could stop after two if they wanted, which they did.

Dad had swept Mom off to a courthouse marriage, followed by a honeymoon swimming in the wholesome mineral waters of Olympia Springs. But the newlyweds ended up living back at Pa's house anyway and going to work for the government.

We lived in the front room, my parents in a high rosewood bed, me on the trundle bed, James on the couch. My mother draped the picture window with heavy lace curtains and a pull-down shade so the whole town wouldn't know our business. A massive armoire took up most of the wall opposite the window. It loomed forward as though any disturbance, like the tensions that simmered between my parents, could cause it to crash down, flattening us. Pa would have to peel us up like cartoon characters.

One morning, as my parents dressed for work, a car pulled in to the driveway and idled for a moment before the engine cut off. Dad parted the curtains and looked out. "Well, looka there," he said. "Didn't think he'd show."

"Now, if we can get Frances in, we'll be in business," my mother said. "Zip this, honey," she said,

Afterheat

in a soft, impatient voice. She was wearing a fitted black wool dress and earrings that flashed beneath her long blond hair.

"All dressed up for Sammy?" Dad asked, pulling the slider tab slowly up her dress.

"What's it to you, soldier?" Mom turned to kiss him, but all she got was one of Dad's tight-lipped kisses. She tried again, but he leaned back.

"Don't touch me," he said, playfully. "You don't know me that well." Dad pulled on silk socks and slid his feet into shoes so highly polished they shone in the half-light coming in through the lace curtains.

A local guy, named Sammy Razor, would be riding to work with them in something called a carpool. My parents worked at the Army Depot in Lexington. Mom was a GS-10, Dad a GS-12. I never understood their conversations about government service ranks or procurement, but I was proud when Mom won the contest for fastest typist in her section. They promoted her to supervisor and excused her from the office on days when they cleaned the typewriters with banana oil. When she was little, she'd eaten a dozen bananas in one sitting and now she couldn't stand the sight of them. We had to keep them on the back porch, because even the smell gave her a sick headache.

CD Collins

James and I watched from the bedroom window as a tall man in a bulky coat climbed into the backseat of our Pontiac, my parents in front, Dad at the wheel. After the taillights disappeared down Antwerp Street, we stampeded into Pa's room, crawled into his bed, and snuggled on either side of him.

"Tell us about the man who fell overboard!" I demanded.

"Yeah," James urged. "Tell us about throwing the buoy."

The goal was to get Pa to say "ship," so we could accuse him of cussing.

"Ship," he'd repeat, good-naturedly, "I said 'ship.'"

Our parents swore continually, but we couldn't draw a curse word out of Pa, no matter how we wore on his patience. He told us tales about the Vanderbilts, who'd saved up their guilders till they could buy a castle and his own adventures in the Navy. Our favorite was the one about Mom eloping from the front porch of this very house. "She made two dates at the carnival," he said, as though he still could not believe it. "And your daddy got here first." He encircled James and me with his long arms and hugged us close.

Pa, dressed in his navy whites, stared out from

Afterheat

the gold-framed photograph on his bureau. Broad-chested and well-groomed, a lady killer, people said. Next to the picture, his cut-glass whiskey decanter sparkled, a string of rock candy dangling inside. Sometimes Pa slipped us bourbon-soaked crystal to suck, the woody bite spreading across our tongues. When his alarm rang, Pa roused us out of bed, got us bathed and dressed, then sent us across the street to Mapleton Elementary, a nickel in our pockets for afternoon milk break. We secretly gave Pa our lunch money, which he deposited in individual passbook accounts with our names on them. The plan was to become rich like the Vanderbilts. At noon, we came home where Pa had our lunch ready—hot tamales, Salisbury steak, whatever we wanted.

When our parents came through the door that evening, I knew something was bad wrong. James and I hopped on the rosewood bed. Dad unknotted his tie and drew it from around his neck, then flung it across the arm of the chair. His suit jacket followed, then slid to the floor. Mom went behind the partition, but instead of changing into her comfortable slacks and blouse, she emerged in her nightgown, and stretched out on the chaise by the window. People called my mother a bombshell; sometimes sunlight breaking over the planes of her face could leave you breathless. I felt that way now, spellbound and frightened, watching her in the lamplight.

"You'll be gone two weeks. What's the big deal?" my mother said, poking a cigarette between her lips and lighting it. "Ten damn days."

Dad got awards for coming up with ideas to streamline government projects, so they were always sending him off to Army bases to explain his suggestions to the generals.

"You can't ride alone with Sammy Razor," Dad said. "I don't buy that bit about his sleeping sickness for a minute."

"We need the cash." Mom blew a plume of smoke toward the ceiling.

Dad narrowed his eyes at Mom as though the mention of money was an assault on his manhood. Though a small man, he dominated a room. He was well-shaped in body and face like those movie star men who look like giants onscreen, but in real life were little like my dad. They all seemed to carry a dangerous streak like a feral cat.

"Sammy got bitten by a tsetse fly in the service," Mom said, tapping her ash into a ceramic ashtray shaped like a geisha girl. "It's a real thing."

Afterheat

"It's bull," Dad said. "He'll have you over on the side of the road screwing."

Mom crushed her cigarette and a thin branch of smoke rose from the geisha's ceramic belly. "I'm sure you'll be providing plenty of stud service down in Fort Benning."

James slid from the bed. "Come on, private," he said to me. "Or I'll put a pineapple under your tail." In the army, they called grenades pineapples, so said my dad.

"Dogface," I answered in army talk.

I followed James into the kitchen where Pa was flouring pork chops, laying them hissing into the skillet. He looked down at us over the tops of his glasses and smiled in a sad way. If he heard my parents, he didn't mention it.

"Fire in the hole," James shouted, grabbing a lemon and pulling an imaginary pin. He lobbed the lemon at me and it rolled across the linoleum floor. Once you pulled the pin, you had to get rid of it fast or it could blow your head off instead of your enemy's. I kicked it back to James, but Pa scooped it up with one of his big, freckled hands.

"I taught you better than this," he scolded. "At least you two know how to behave. Now go on out so

I can get this dinner cooked." He shooed us into his room, where James' train was set up in front of the gas fire.

To drown out my parents, James switched on his train set full blast. I opened the window seat and pulled out my art box—sheets of Pa's typing paper and colored pencils—Blendwell, they were called, Periwinkle, Carnation, Forest Green. I drew fireworks and roosters, daisies and daggers, whatever struck my fancy.

I smoothed out a sheet and sketched an outline of the house Dad worked on every weekend, a new house for us, supposedly, though I had no intention of leaving Pa. Coloring in a grid of bricks, I thought about how you could say 'screws' and 'studs' if you were talking about building, but not about people. Then there was stud service, which Mom accused Dad of giving and Dad accused Mom of receiving. This service could apparently get you on a fast track to hell.

I copied a diagram from *Life* magazine that showed atoms with busy electrons running in minuscule patterns. If you divided one, it set off a bigger explosion than you could imagine in a hundred years. I imagined my parents' words floated through the house like those radioactive isotopes, settling all

Afterheat
around us, glowing along the arms of the couch.

That Saturday, while Dad was gone to Fort Benning, Pa took James and me to a movie about a giant moth with two tiny Japanese daughters who sang in a special language for their mother to rescue them. The movie scared me so much that I tried to find James in the huge darkened film house. I ended up running out into the lobby where Pa was bent over the popcorn, fluffing it up. He drew me a Coke, stirred in chocolate syrup, and set it on the glass counter.

"Why don't you sit up here?" Pa steadied his tall, wooden stool while I climbed up.

The glass magnified the boxes of candy from above, the way Pa's eyeglasses magnified his eyes. The thick edges of the counter had a green cast to them like the hollow of an ocean wave. I rested a forefinger in one of the deep chips while I sucked the sweet carbonation through the straw.

When I looked up, Pa's eyes were welled up with tears.

"Your daddy's house is almost finished," he said.

I nodded and looked down. Through the glass, the candy bars looked enormous—shaggy, coconut-covered Zagnuts; soft-crusted Sugar Babies; snow-capped Nonpareils. Pa's whiskey-soaked crystals were better. There'd be no rock candy where we were moving, I was pretty sure.

One morning deep into winter, Pa called for us to come look. James and I rushed outside into air so cold the wind froze the moisture and whipped tiny ice needles against our faces. The snow lay blue and deep on the lawn, solid enough that even Pa did not punch through. Near the horizon, streams of green, indigo, and silver flared up and fanned above us. The lights waved and trembled in supernatural hues.

"Maybe it's a flying saucer," James said. "Aliens come to Earth."

Pa wore his striped pajamas and slippers and stared transfixed into the sky. "Children," he said. "Remember this. The only time you'll ever get to see the Northern Lights." He arranged the thin wires of his spectacles, his pale mouth dropped open.

Even after James and I stole back inside to warm our hands by the gas fire, Pa lingered like a man hypnotized. When he finally came in, his lips were blue, his hands a terrible white. He poured himself a shot of bourbon and sank into his rocking chair. We climbed onto his lap, but he'd taken a chill so deep that

Afterheat

no amount of hand rubbing or cheek pinching could get him warm.

Now, on dark mornings, James and I wait in front of the Crystal Inn on Main Street. My mother had waited tables there in high school, so she asked one of her former co-workers to keep an eye on us till the bus picked us up. At the new school, I fell into a habit of placing a period after each word as I wrote. I knew better, but I couldn't help it. I thought there was a bug in my hair, so I pulled out one hair at a time until I caused bald spots on the back of my head.

The wide, starch-fed waitress swung open the door of the restaurant, allowing a steam cloud to billow into the frigid air. "Come in off the street," she hollered. "Big truck come along, you'll be nothing but little greasy spots."

James liked spinning on the barstools and eating biscuits and gravy with the farmers, but I wanted to be outside in the black morning, gazing up at the stars. Pa was there, I knew, somewhere in the Milky Way. "Ana no kawa," he'd taught me. "The Japanese call it the River of Heaven." I felt like it was my fault that Pa had caught pneumonia because James and I hadn't brought him back inside. But Mom told me that it wasn't pneumonia that took him, but his lymph, a fluid that flows around your body, cleaning up. They said his sickness had been with him a long time. When he'd stopped breathing in the hospital, Mom had done mouth-to-mouth resuscitation till the nurses pulled her off him.

For months, the farmers talked about how they'd seen the aurora borealis as they'd gone about their milking and throwing down hay. Late-shift factory workers had seen it too, walking to their cars in the dark. Some thought it marked the end of the world. But it looked to me like the world had kept on going, whether I liked it or not.

I would read years later that the Northern Lights were connected to the intensity of solar flares. Pa had been right—the event was historic because the lights were visible so far south. I learned that the lights are caused by the glow of atoms as they are hit by speeding protons and electrons. An enormous geomagnetic storm generates the image of the aurora with cathode rays and produces an effect like an unfathomably large TV tube projected upon the upper atmosphere. They were not, as Pa had said, sunlight refracted from the polar snow, like a rainbow.

In the bomb over Hiroshima, the trigger that sparked the resulting nuclear fission was a collision between the nucleus of an atom of uranium and a neutron. For each atom of uranium that split, three more neutrons were produced. If the lump of uranium is big enough, a critical mass, these neutrons go on to split more atoms, causing a chain reaction and creating energy in the form of heat and light.

Chapter 4
Lalique

In a small town, there is trust in the person across the table, the other side of the cash register, the other end of the phone line. If I say I'll be back with your money this afternoon, you know I'll be back, purely because I say I will. Because you know my daddy and my cousins. You know you're going to share the same God's acre until Kingdom Come.

But there is also mistrust of the person across the table, because he knows your daddy and your cousins. You can never escape him. You can never have anything just to yourself without having to hide it. And it is this inside, hidden part where things can fester, especially at night, especially with drink.

Although no one said so, you tried to follow

Afterheat

a blueprint for living well in Vance, Kentucky, in the 1960s. You bought a speedboat. You bought water skis. You packed fried chicken, potato salad, and deviled eggs in a cooler, and you drove to Red River on a Sunday, cruising down the Mountain Parkway in your big, shiny car. You ate at the Carousel Lounge, where you could have a tall, cold beer on a Saturday night. One, two, or one too many. It was the place where you believed you could have the best time and the place where that good time could turn.

    Everybody in town has some association with the lounge's dark interior. My aunt met her future husband in there, stepped in on a lark to escape the sun and noise of the Easter Parade. She claimed that as soon as her eyes adjusted, she'd seen him staring at her from the back booth. "Fate," she always said, no matter how pitiful he became as a husband. "No way to resist." When Trixie Hayes was too drunk to cook, Mr. Hayes took their girls on down to the Carousel Lounge. The owner, Dallas Starr, operated the cash register. He bragged about campaigning for that old Dixiecrat Happy Chandler while he worked his wife and daughter like field hands. Since the election, Dallas hadn't lifted a finger, except to take people's money. He even took IOUs, stacking the receipts in a cigar box. He knew people were good for it and if they weren't, he understood that, too.

Dallas ran a tight ship. No drunks, no fights, or he'd set you on the sidewalk. You could decide for yourself whether to go home where you belonged or else swagger on down to the Alibi Club, where they opened their doors to anybody and where you might get yourself shot just for asking a lady to dance.

The dinners tasted good at the Carousel Lounge, catfish and hush puppies, T-bone steaks with Diego salad, homemade cream pies. They served lamb fries with white gravy, too, and if you don't know what that is, well, just try some first. All the booths had individual jukeboxes, red-and-white checked tablecloths where your husband might be talking confidentially to someone nestled back in the shadows.

One night, Mom called to check if Dad was down at the Carousel. I squatted on the kitchen floor lacing up my shoes, but I could hear Mr. Starr through the receiver. "Hey, Junior. Are you here?" he called. While Mom waited, strains of Hank Williams whined up out of the jukebox. Then Dallas said, "Sorry, hon. I guess he just left."

Mom jammed the phone into its wall cradle

Afterheat

and stared out the window above the sink. I could tell Mr. Starr burned Mom up, always covering for Dad. But I didn't blame Mr. Starr for anything.

"Should we go down there?" I asked her.

Mom shook her head no without looking at me. Then, still dressed in her fancy work clothes, she picked up the electric mixer and clicked the silver beaters into place.

"Going for a bike ride," I said, opening the door to the garage, letting our dog, Flip, swish into the kitchen so he wouldn't follow me.

"Don't be late for supper," she said with a weariness that made me hate Dad.

I mounted my English racer boy-style, swinging one leg over the seat, peddling as fast as I could up the first hill, then sailed down, my hair flying back, my arms spread wide. On one side of the road, fields of winter wheat shone the velvety green of crème de menthe; on the other, an orchard of pear trees bloomed white.

I missed Pa, but it seemed like nobody but James and me even noticed he was gone. We kept his old briefcase in the attic of the new house out on Cream Alley Road, the key hidden up in the eaves. Inside, candles, strings of rock candy, a pair of mother-of-pearl cufflinks, a sterling silver flask engraved with Pa's initials. The flask was empty, but whiskey vapors welled up when we unscrewed the cap. We stored his pocket watch in a leather pouch, drawing it out to watch the gears moving through the glass back. Seventeen tiny jewels. We wound the stem gently back and forth, the way Pa taught us.

We were country people now. Dad brought home a flop-eared German Shepherd puppy. We named him Flip and he loped after James all over the Kennedys' fields. I had my own lavender room with a canopied bed, a real closet, and a chest of drawers made from solid cherry. James' room was at the other end of the house, across from my parents, the floor furnace in between. He supposedly got the warm room because he was older, but I knew it was because he was the boy.

Mom bought an upright piano. Her sinewy fingers dashed along the keys as James and I sang along "I got my bags. I got my reservation. I spent each dime I could afford…" Melodies floated out the screened windows into the clean air. Mom picked out a gold-and-white bedroom suite in a style she called French Provincial, furnished the living room with an aqua sectional couch and sheer, tangerine drapes. She displayed her Bohemian art glass and Art Nouveau vases on the partition of shelves that divided the living room and dining room. Her prize, a Lalique bowl, occupied its own shelf. Pa had brought her with him to auctions and shown her how to tell real items from fake. She'd watched his bidding techniques, flared nostrils or a raised eyebrow, letting the auctioneer know that he was in, but not people he was bidding against. She'd caught the bug for it, too. Certain things were just too beautiful to let go, but she never told us what they cost.

I whipped my bike around, just as Mrs. Kennedy crested the hill in her maroon Thunderbird, honking without slowing down. James and I thought that Mrs. Kennedy would just as soon run us over as look at us. Vanessa Van Dough we called her. I braced against the slipstream of her car, turning my head to keep the grit out of my eyes. The Kennedys might own the fields, but it didn't stop James and me from building tree houses in the mock orange trees or licking the cow's salt blocks.

I pedaled slowly home as the sun sank into an orange bar, melting into the farthest ridge. When Dad went missing, he could usually be found down at the Carousel. What he was up to was a mystery—an affair, maybe, or some dubious financial transactions. Bad dealings, whatever they were, matters that had to be kept out of the papers. Mom wanted to get to the bottom of it, so James and I often rode with her far out in the county to check names on mailboxes. Or we'd wait in the car outside the Lounge, "Gonna crash his little party," she'd say, checking herself in the rear view mirror while she smoothed on lipstick.

Tonight, I saw our Pontiac parked at a crooked angle in the driveway. A poisonous fear clutched at me as I ditched my bike in the yard and yanked open the door. I found them in the kitchen, Mom cornering Dad between the counter and the stove.

"Been out getting something strange?" She poked him hard in the chest with a forefinger.

"None of your business." His words sounded jumbled as though his tongue were frozen. He gripped the counter's edge to brace himself. His normally smooth, wavy hair stood up in haphazard chunks.

He turned his back to Mom, rummaged in the cabinet and pulled out his box of Stanback headache powders. He unfolded the wax paper and let the fine crystals slide into his mouth. He chased the powder with water. I got out of his way as he lurched past me into the living room and switched on *The Huntley-*

Afterheat
Brinkley Report.

Mom followed him, ravening like a fox. "Who is she? Who is the whore?"

James' radio played softly behind his door. Dad had built our house solid—red brick with a concrete basement and a glassed-in sun porch. Shade trees in front, big fenced-in yard in back. But when he came home warped with drink, it set off a quaking, a shuddering so deep that it felt like eyes, souls, and fingernails were at stake. Sometimes, James and I closed the door to my bedroom and played Three Stooges as loud as we could. We took turns being Moe, socking each other in the kisser, while we thrashed around on my canopied bed. We laughed when we got hurt, because we knew our turn was coming soon.

But tonight I stayed put behind the shelf partition, listening. I'd throw myself between them if it came to blows.

"Maybe it's just the bottle." Mom kept on. "Are you really just a mean old drunk like your father?"

Dad ignored her, leaning back in his easy chair and concentrating on the news. The anchors traded comments about Nikita Khrushchev and John Kennedy.

"Answer me!" Mom shouted. "What's so

damned important that you can't be bothered to come home?"

With that question, she probably reminded herself of other nights he'd come home late or drunk, even Saturdays, even Christmas Eve. Her sadness seemed to break her then, bowing her shoulders, and dragging down the corners of her mouth as she returned to the kitchen.

At dinner, I mistakenly began the 23rd psalm instead of the short grace.

"The Lord is my shepherd; I shall not want…"

"Stop," Dad said, but it was a sin to stop a prayer.

"He maketh me to lie down in green pastures," I chanted faster into my clasped hands.

Dad's fist hit the dining room table, pounded again and again, rattling the heavy rose-patterned plates and making the silverware jump. I shut my eyes. When I opened them, I saw the shiny tines of a fork plunging into Mom's wrists as she stabbed herself, four, eight, twelve blood points rising. My mind raced to my Cadette Scout first-aid manual—how to treat a puncture wound.

James disappeared into the bathroom and returned with a bottle of hydrogen peroxide and fistful

Afterheat

of tissues. Mom fixed her eyes on Dad, who picked up the meatloaf platter, chose a slice, and passed the plate to me.

Our parents carpooled to work at five o'clock every morning, leaving James and me the whole house to wreck. On the shelves, Mom's antique glass caught wedges of morning sun. James and I practiced our cursing while we hurled shoes and baseballs. Before the bus came, we rushed to clean it all up, and let Flip out into the backyard. We waited to be picked up under the full, green crown of the wild cherry tree.

One afternoon shortly before school let out for the summer, James and I barreled into the house. We planned to change out of our school clothes into our roughhouse clothes and play baseball down at the Spencers. Instead, we found Flip reared back on his haunches in the living room, looking up at us quizzically.

"God help us," James said, realizing we'd left him in the house all day.

I had the sensation of a steel hand pressing on my chest, a throat-catching dread as I surveyed the house. The overstuffed couch pillows gaped open, their fuzzy innards tumbled out. The tangerine drapes hung in tatters; bananas and plums from the fruit bowl formed crazy impasto patterns on the carpet. I followed a trail of frosted Angel food cake from the kitchen into our parents' bedroom where I found half-buried bits among the unmade satin sheets. Mom's bowl with the dancing women lay burst into a dozen pieces on the hardwood floor. I picked up a luminous shard, part of an arm and tiny outstretched hand.

"Lalique," I said.

James and I stared at each other in horror. We knew we'd bruised her very heart—our alluring mother, high-strung and preoccupied, lover of high fashion, fine furniture, and handsome men.

"We're going straight to the orphanage," I said.

"Don't worry," James said. "We'll be dead."

"Damn chicken punk," I accused him.

"Shit-assed polecat," he hissed back.

With brooms and the garden rake we cleaned up as best we could, then slunk to our separate rooms. First, the heavy clunk of a car door closing and the fading hum of an engine as her ride drove away, then the creak of the front door, footsteps treading slowly room to room. I wildly surveyed my collection of dolls from around the world lined up on my dresser. I made out the sound of rummaging in the hall closet, followed by metallic clicks. She was loading Dad's shotgun. James must have heard it, too.

By the time we arrived in the yard, Mom had already tucked the gun's stock against her right shoulder and was sighting Flip down the barrel. We flanked her legs, hugging them, pleading for his life.

"It's our fault!"

"He's just a puppy."

Flip did not approach us, but sat whimpering. When Mom cocked the hammer, he tilted his head at the sound, ears flopping.

"Mark, set, go," James murmured. We rushed toward Flip, James falling to his knees embracing him, me kneeling in front.

"Get the hell out of the way," Mom shouted, motioning with the barrel. "If I take him to the pound. They'll shoot him anyway."

We didn't move a muscle. My parents sawed heads from open-eyed fish, sent squirrels plummeting to the ground with a .22 rifle. Kittens had disappeared. I knew Mom was perfectly capable, but I would have rather died in the mud than watch Flip pumped full of buckshot. Go ahead and shoot, I thought, half-wishing she would, picturing myself face down in the yard.

This is the scene Dad witnessed as he pulled

into the drive, the tires skidding into the grass. He leapt out, leaving the car bouncing on its springs. When Mom turned her head to look at Dad, James grabbed a stick and hurled it as far into the backyard as he could. Flip bounded after it. Dad approached Mom with care, his arms extended, and she laid the shotgun across them.

Kneeling in my mud-streaked dress, I wondered if Pa watched down on us from heaven. Dad pulled the bolt back, broke the gun open. He withdrew the two bulky red and brass cartridges and slid them into his pants pockets.

"Come on, honey," he said holding out a hand to Mom. She didn't take it, but she headed for the house.

James and I waited by the door while Dad took it all in, the ruined couch, the ribboned curtains. In the failing light, the carpet looked almost normal. Dad drew an Andy Williams from its sleeve and lowered it into the stereo console. At first all we could hear was Flip yapping at something in the backyard, then the needle swung into its groove and music flowed from the speakers. Dad pulled Mom close, swaying to "There's a summer place..." the singer's voice smooth as a flower petal. Over Dad's shoulder, Mom's eyes

Afterheat
softened and seemed to lose focus.

"Daddy gave me that bowl for my twenty-first birthday," she said to no one in particular. "It was one of a kind."

In Hiroshima, the displaced atomic mass manifested itself as a fireball 5400 degrees Fahrenheit at its core. It pushed air out as it expanded, creating a fiery wind. As it rose, the air rushed back in, sucking up dust and rubble to form a cloud in the shape of a Death Angel mushroom.

Chapter 5
The Carousel Lounge

Saturday nights my family ate dinner at the Carousel. Mom would have rather stayed home, but Dad liked to socialize. People we knew were less casual back then, dressed to align ourselves with the class we were rising into, not the one we were leaving behind. Sports jackets and creased trousers and expertly ironed dresses were what we wore for a simple drive in the country.

Sixties women were curvy, the men, lean. As farmers and carpenters, they worked, not worked out. Nights out, my father's hair gleamed with pomade, my mother's blond mane whipped into a variety of ringlets, turrets, and waves. She visited these afflictions on me as well; a permed tomboy is a pathetic sight.

One Saturday morning in June, I worked at the

Afterheat

kitchen table, snapping the ends from half-runner beans and zipping out the tough string. My grandmother had taught me how to string beans on her front porch, to be careful not to break off too much and waste good food. After I filled the white enamel basin, Mom rinsed the beans and put them on to boil.

Time moved slowly back then, and there was plenty of it. Time for grooming; time for conversation. Country women kept up with the news through party lines; ten or twelve houses with the same number lowered the price. You could pick up the phone anytime and join the conversation. Dad insisted that we have a private line, but he swore that my Mom could talk for an hour to a wrong number.

Saturday mornings, Carmen Gray visited without fail. Tall and full-busted with a gap between her front teeth, Carmen always had a deep suntan by April.

"Morning, sleeping beauties!" she exclaimed, stealing through the back door and ambushing us in the kitchen.

"Oh hush," Mom answered. "I've been up since seven o'clock. Picking beans before it got too hot." She tore a slice of salt-risen toast and handed me the good burnt part.

CD Collins

"Well, that was smart. It's supposed to hit a hundred today!" Carmen shouted. "Where's that Claytis? Wonder if he's got any work for Buster coming up."

Mom told Carmen that Dad had run over to the new hardware store. "It's over by the old Kroger's," she explained, "Between Hiler's Body Shop and the Mill. Probably picking up a six-pack at Big Fred's while he's at it."

"Oh Lord, I'll bet you a silver dollar that Buster is with him," Carmen said, pursing her lips and nodding. She turned and left, letting the screen door slam.

"We're going out to the Carousel tonight if you all want to come down," Mom hollered after her.

Full disclosure of a person's whereabouts was expected. Ditto inviting oneself to dinner. You never heard the words "appropriate" or "boundary," or "carcinogenic," for that matter, as we doused our gardens with DDT.

We lived our daily lives under a rainbow of trust in the future. Dad had big dreams and he didn't mind working hard for them. He also liked to have a good time. Like his father before him, this required a bottle. You had your Miller High Life; you had your

Afterheat
barrel-aged Bourbon.

I dreaded dinners at the Carousel Lounge as much as I looked forward to them. Despite Dallas' best efforts, come Saturday night if the evening would end with couples jitterbugging and kissing on the dance floor or with curses and gunfire was anybody's guess.

A little while before we left, I'd appeared in the kitchen in jean shorts and one of James' worn-out shirts with the sleeves torn off. "Well, shit, Ruby," Mom said. "Wear what you want. I'm too tired to fight you." She lifted the last quart of green beans out of the boiler and set it on the counter with the other twenty. All afternoon, the jars had made a sucking snap that meant they'd been sealed. Defeated by guilt, I changed into a yellow sundress, matching anklets, and patent leather shoes. I couldn't even run in this getup. If I died trying to escape Jack the Ripper, it'd be her fault.

We headed for the Lounge early that evening for the sake of air conditioning as much as for dinner.

"Fresh bass tonight," Wendy said, positioning the carbon on the green pad. Wendy was Dallas and Marbury Starr's daughter, moved here from Virginia. To us Vance natives, driving to the next county was like entering foreign territory, so Virginia may as well have been the moon. Dark-haired and olive skinned, Wendy looked like an enchanting forest creature.

"How about bass dinners all around?" Dad said.

"With French fries!" James said.

"Baked potato for me," Mom said, closing her menu.

"I'll have a Miller on tap," Dad added and Wendy went to fetch it.

The red leather booth felt cool under my legs. A plastic replica of an eternally foaming beer revolved on the wall above us, washing our faces in gold. Over by the bar, Buster and Carmen Gray swilled highballs. Buster worked odd jobs for my father. He was so proud of Carmen, whom he'd met on a highway job down in New Orleans. He claimed to have proposed to her on the spot, and brought her along with her son, Frankie, up to Vance. Dad called Frankie a bastard, but when I repeated the term, I got my legs switched with a willow branch.

While we waited for our dinners, Dad gave us money to play Space Creatures pinball. I handed Wendy the dollar and watched fascinated as she thumbed the metal levers of the coin dispenser strapped around her waist. I was in fifth grade, Wendy in ninth, high school.

"There you go, honey," Wendy said. When she placed the coins in my cupped hands, it felt like a little

Afterheat

electric wave shimmering up my arms. A shadowy, fleeting surprise, like heat lightning. I looked down and forgot to thank her.

James worked the flippers fast and expertly, making the space ships flash and ding. I was terrible at pinball, so I gave James the rest of the quarters and I climbed up on a barstool to watch the cooks. Wendy waited tables and served drinks, while her mother, Marbury, worked the cold side: chopping carrots and lettuce for salads, kneading dough for yeast rolls. Lady Delilah, an imposing, curvaceous black woman, headed the cooking crew, making sure the steaks were precision-grilled and the oil was up to temperature for the hissing baskets of hush puppies and thick, meal-rubbed catfish the cooks lowered into the Fryolator.

"This better be right hot," Delilah hollered to Floyd Jack, her helper. "I don't want 'em coming out heavy." She leaned over the vat of oil to check the speed of the bubbles. "I can't abide a greasy fish."

"Don't Delilah's backside have a life of its own?" Floyd Jack remarked to Big Al, maybe louder than he meant, because all of us at the bar heard him.

"Keep on…" Delilah warned him as she heaved a sack of cornmeal onto the counter with her big chestnut-colored arms. She slit open the fifty-pound sack with one smooth motion of her butcher knife. You wouldn't cross Delilah on a dare.

While Wendy, Marbury, Lady Delilah, and her crew labored like dray horses, all Mr. Starr did was stand at the cash register and yammer. Someone at the bar called for a beer and Mr. Starr called back, "What do you think I've got waitresses in here for?" and kept right on talking.

Marbury wiped her hands on her apron and pulled a beer for the man, setting it on the bar in front of him. "You know how he is," she said, with as convincing a smile as she could muster. She had such a head of curly hair, you could barely see her face. I watched her fingers slide expertly along a carrot, slicing rounds as thin as a dime.

Delilah glanced over at me and fished some hush puppies from the Fryolator. She tossed them sizzling into a basket lined with waxed paper. "Skinny little thing," she teased, setting the basket in front of me.

I ate the hush puppies one by one, tossing them between my fingers to cool them, then pulled a napkin from the dispenser and wiped the grease from my hands.

Mr. Starr was whooping it up with some

Afterheat
customers, so I stood up and waved to get his attention.

"What can I do for you, Miss Ruby?" he said, slapping a hand on the bar for emphasis.

"Ladies' room, please."

I could feel Mr. Starr watching me as I walked to the locked door. I wished I weren't too old for Mom to escort me down. The Lounge had two long staircases, one leading to the Starrs' apartment above the restaurant, the other to the restrooms in the basement. I heard the staticky buzz and quickly turned the knob. Once the door locked behind me, I clutched the handrail and descended the steps one at a time in my despised slick-bottomed patent-leather shoes. I wanted real shoes with gripping soles like the boys. I wanted overalls and T-shirts, not stiff, frilly dresses that cut at my thighs with little lacy teeth.

The stairs were smooth and off plumb, painted gray like the walls and low ceiling. I descended and found my way along the corridor to the gray door. As with long afternoons in the dentist's chair, I sensed time stretch and prolong. I breathed in the thick antiseptic-laden air and unfurled toilet tissue from its roll on the jury-rigged wire. The high whiz of the dentist's drill, the crazy-house basement of the Carousel Lounge, the shudder inside our house, maybe those were what was true, flying wide-armed on my bicycle into the cherry-flavored dusk, running free in Kennedy Fields, a dream.

I made quick work washing my hands, then clattered half-panicked back up the stairs, pushing through into the cool of the restaurant.

"Somebody's going to crack their head on those stairs one day," my father said as I slid into the booth beside my mother.

My parents appeared to be ready to launch one of their wrangles about Dad's drinking, his eyes red as he signaled for another beer.

"Man needs to relax," he said, avoiding my mother's tight look.

Across the restaurant, Wendy sashayed around the oilcloth-covered tables, leaning over into the booths and letting herself be teased.

"Poor little thing," Mom said, clinking the ice in her highball with a rocking motion of her wrist. What she meant was that Wendy was the kind of girl you could take one look at and know where she was headed.

The town projected a bad end onto her with the force of a curse. Too pretty, not from here. They predicted a quick crash in a speeding hot rod or

Afterheat

disappearance into a swamp out in Fox Run. Maybe some drake would swoop down upon her, then fly away. She'd live above the Carousel with her baby or else move into a shack over on Mitchell Street and never amount to anything. "Bless her heart," people said, because they'd seen it all before.

When we were halfway through dinner, Buster raised his glass toward our table, and Dad held up his beer. This meant they were headed for bigger things tonight. Wendy walked by carrying a tray full of cocktails. She glanced over at us with a knowing look.

As James and I argued over a slice of coconut crème pie we were splitting, Buster pulled up a chair at the end of the booth and leaned forward to light my mother's cigarette. He had a beefy build, a stomach that rolled over his pants so you couldn't see his belt, and little pinpoint diamond eyes.

"Go for a ride?" he said to Dad. "Heard they got a new batch out on Harper's Ridge."

A batch meant moonshine, 180 proof corn liquor, so strong they sometimes had to water it down to keep the essence from floating away as vapor.

Carmen sidled up and hugged Buster from behind. "Mmm mmm," she half-scolded him. The gap between her front teeth was exaggerated by her mouth being almost always open, smiling and laughing, eating and drinking.

My mother took a long inhale. "Just drop me and the kids off," she said to my father through her smoky exhale. "If you're home past midnight, I'm bolting the door."

"Oh, come on, honey," Dad said. "Let's just run get a pint. We could use a little relaxation tonight."

"Come on, pretty lady," Carmen said to Mom. "Kids don't have school tomorrow. Let's do a little carrying on."

"Little nightcap back at the house," Dad promised.

"One drink," Mom said. "Back at the house."

We followed Buster to his car. "Plenty of room in the Olds," he said, unlocking the doors. We bunched in, men in front, women in back, and went speeding out toward Camargo. Buster headed down one fork in the road, then another, passing barns and silos that seemed to rise up suddenly from the hills. He slowed as we bumped along a dirt road, and then parked the car behind a small frame house. The men went inside, James too. The trees filtered light from the crescent moon, illuminating the eyes of a few night creatures that stole past the plywood carport. The sound of frogs

Afterheat

and cicadas pulsed in the humid night air, which flowed in through the rolled-down windows.

The men emerged from the house and gathered in a circle. I could see them lighting something in a can, a blue flame rising. Then Dad pulled out his wallet and handed something to one of the men. Buster tossed Dad the keys, then lugged the big jug to the car.

Dad gunned out of the drive, sending up a spray of gravel. "Hand me that jug," Dad said.

"Don't you dare," my mother warned.

"Oh, Buster, let's just wait," Carmen cajoled. She pulled me onto her lap and held me around the waist with her strong arms.

The double yellow lines meant do not pass, but with a flick of his wrist, Dad crossed the oncoming lane in front of a big farm truck and drove into the shallow ditch. The Oldsmobile lurched and thumped over the uneven ground.

"Good Lord, Junior," Buster said, grasping the dashboard.

James crawled into the back seat beside Mom, who leaned forward to slap the back of Dad's head. Dizzily, I clung to Carmen's arms. She pulled me tighter, whispering into my hair that everything was going to be okay.

"I really am very thirsty," Dad said, calmly.

"Oh, a little swaller never hurt," Buster said and slapped the jug into my father's waiting hand.

My father slowed, pulled the car up out of the ditch, the front fender churning up sparks on the asphalt road before it tore off and tumbled heavily away, like a struck animal. James craned his neck to watch it roll away. A caravan of cars full of teenagers whizzed by, arms and screaming heads sticking out the windows, radio blasting into the night. Dad cradled the jug in his arm, took a long draw, then drove on.

Back in town, Dad pulled up next to our car, still parked outside the Lounge. Mom hopped out, ordering James and me into the Pontiac.

"Where you going?" Dad asked, pretending innocence.

"Get a good look," Mom said, ducking her face down to meet him eye to eye. "Because it's the last time you'll ever see any of us again."

Mom didn't slow down till we pulled into a Jerry's Drive-In in Lexington. "Black coffee," she said into the speaker. "And two Cokes."

"We could go to Louisville and ride the riverboat," James said.

"This is an emergency," I informed him. "Not a

Afterheat
vacation."

We could stay with Pa's sister, June, down in Florida, I offered, or live in Uncle Skeeter's cabin on Chalk Lake. Mom didn't answer, so we quietly worked on our drinks. Maybe Wendy Starr would visit me at the Chalk Lake, swim alongside me in the cool, green water. We'd do perfect jackknives from the board and sun ourselves on the wooden dock.

Both of Wendy's parents drank, too. Maybe Wendy could explain why my Dad's thinking got unstrung as he sipped from those frosted glasses. Secretly, I looked up to her—Wendy with her deep-set slanted eyes, half-hidden behind her auburn hair. I wanted to ask her questions. What was my Dad up to when we weren't there? Did she believe in God? I wanted to possess her quick grace, to run away with her to whatever exotic forest she'd come from.

We stayed in the car at Jerry's Drive-In until our breaths misted the windshield over, our Cokes drained, the melting ice chunks sucked up through our straws. Even the late-night teenagers had all scratched off in their jalopies.

Abruptly, Mom dropped her lit cigarette onto the parking lot and turned the ignition switch. She drove the Pontiac straight home, but Dad wasn't there.

Sometime later, I woke to the sound of him pounding furiously on the door. "Let me in! Let me in my own damn house."

I listened to their tangled voices, rising, settling, then the sound of crickets coming in through the window. It was like that in my family; no matter what happened, blood and broken glass, my mother's curses and tears or my father's prolonged silences, we all ended up in our beds at night, Mom and Dad in the French Provincial room, my brother across in his spool bed, his action figures in a heap on the floor.

We'd been so close to leaving, driving far away. Why had Mom come back? I supposed we weren't enough, James and me. I was not enough. I pressed my head deep into my pillow and longed ferociously for Pa.

Against Pa's wishes, Mom had enrolled me in school when I was four. She told them I was seven, but I was so small they had to build a block for my feet to keep me from sliding out of the desk onto the varnished floors. Hardly able to grip a crayon, I got an F in coloring. From then on, it seemed, the world was too big for me, full of mysterious code.

On the way to my grandmother's farm, I read

road signs that said Do Not Pass or Pass With Care, which I misread to say Pass With Car. A sign on the grassy median read Seedlings Do Not Mow. I folded this message into my deepest heart: Seedlings Do Not Know.

Back then, I did not question the tangled, magnolia-scented world I inhabited. My father's long absences, my mother's white-eyed rage. Like watching the Hollywood dramas my mother took me to see, I absorbed the weight of the passions around me, which I could feel but not interpret. People stepped out on each other; deals needed to be cut. I couldn't tell if my parents were on the same side or if they were enemies.

Our preacher, Reverend Colley, drove an MG. His wife wore orange lipstick and hugged me like the orphan she took me to be. From the pulpit, he told stories where men dreamed of fatted calves and smuggled gold in grain sacks from the king's palace; bony and bearded, a wise man raised his staff and the sea divided, stood up in a corridor of mighty waves.

The morning after the moonshine run, I walked to the Baptist church at the end of the road. I washed my face and shoved my hair back with a plastic headband and wore the same yellow dress I'd worn the night before. After church, I tacked a notice on my door:

> *Do Not Enter*
> *The Sin of God*

I believed I had written "The Sign of God." I wanted to summon a power beyond myself that could fend off Little Eeka the Snake Eater, Jack the Ripper, thieves who stole children through their bedroom windows. My parents found my mistake hilarious. Ruby Clay Chambers, the sin of God.

Afterheat

Chapter 6
Heat

James and I rode in the rear-facing seat of the station wagon flying down Indian Fields Road, towing the Bonaventures' new speedboat. Riding backward with my feet out the back window made me feel dizzy in a good way. Mr. Bonaventure drove too fast on the straight parts of the road and stomped the brakes through the sharp back-road curves. The boat shimmied and bumped, and Mrs. Bonaventure kept warning him to slow down.

"My husband's a maniac, in case you haven't noticed," she half-shouted to Mom, who sat in the middle seat with the two Bonaventure babies.

Mom hoisted the baby boy onto her lap. As she flapped his arms, he screwed his fat face into a baby laugh. His wispy black hair stuck straight up from his head like a troll. "He can floor it for all I care," Mom said.

When I turned to rummage in the middle seat for the bottle of suntan lotion, I caught a glimpse of Mr. Bonaventure's eyes in the rearview mirror. His light-flecked eyes reminded me of the crackled marbles James and I fried in a skillet once as a science experiment. Mr. Bonaventure jammed the brakes again and woke the little girl, who kicked her little roly-poly legs. In a baby-talk voice, Mom explained to her that life was full of surprises like that and she might as well get used to it.

"I mean it," Mrs. Bonaventure scolded. "You'll get us all killed."

Jiggling his eyebrows like Groucho Marx, Mr. Bonaventure began to sing in a theatrical baritone, "Hit the road, Jack, and don't you come back no more, no more, no more, no more..." Mrs. Bonaventure shook her head like she thought he was crazy but sang along with him anyway, her red see-through scarf flapping out the opened window.

Usually, James and I had to split one Coke between us—one divided, the other got first choice. Teaspoons and eyedroppers were involved. But today, we each had our own Coke plus a bag of Tom's Salted

Afterheat

Peanuts and we were headed to Red River. We would picnic on country ham sandwiches and cole slaw and dive off the sandstone rocks down the river from the noisy baby beach.

That's what Mom had promised when she got me out of bed this morning. It was the Sunday before Labor Day, and as I pulled on my faded red swimsuit, I figured it would be the last time we'd go swimming this year. Excited, I pulled the straps over my shoulders and searched my room for my beach towel. Swimming was my absolute favorite thing to do. James wore his swim trunks beneath long pants. He wore long pants all summer no matter how hot it got. It was just the way he was.

While the Bonaventures sang, James pulled a Hershey bar out of his pocket and broke off half for me. I held one of the squares in my mouth, felt the waxy edges lose their shape and sink into a smooth puddle on my tongue. James could be a good brother when he took the notion.

September was even hotter than August had been and the hay fields whizzing by us on either side vibrated with the shrill sawing of locusts. According to Dad, the larvae had been sleeping under the ground for seventeen years in preparation. They crawled up out of the ground without even mouth parts and drummed their breast armor. After we passed a grove of teeming trees, the view opened to fields of alfalfa and silos full of corn.

Dad had been gone all week, off to Texas on Delta Air Lines for a special government assignment. He always wore a dark, pressed suit whenever he flew on planes. In my scrapbook, I'd taped a picture of Dad next to a machine covered in dials. I liked his look of cool concentration as he twirled them, like he understood the reason for everything.

"Which way is Texas?" I asked James.

"That way," he said, pointing left, toward the water tower. "South, southwest." James always had an answer, right or wrong. He took a giant swig of his Coke and then poured his peanuts into the bottle, corked the lip with his thumb, and shook hard.

As James uncorked his bottle, releasing a small geyser of creamy bubbles, I heard the deep boom. I stared at James, his mouth clamped over the bottle, foam spewing from the corners of his lips, and we burst out laughing.

All summer, jets had broken the sound barrier, bouncing plates on the dining room table, rattling the storm doors. This boom was followed by a roar, the air

Afterheat

darkened, and a shower of dirt clods and stones pelted the top of the car. Mr. Bonaventure braked hard as a rock the size of a wheelbarrow landed on the station wagon's hood, killing the engine.

"Oh my God, it's the Russians!" Mrs. Bonaventure's voice was high and piercing.

Mr. Bonaventure turned the key, but the car made a groaning sound.

"Dammit," he growled. "Dammit all to hell." Mrs. Bonaventure shook her head like it was caught in a swarm of bees and both babies began to cry.

"They're bombing Lexington Army Depot," Mom said, searching fiercely out the dusty side windows. "God knows what they've got buried there."

Mr. Bonaventure jumped out of the car and glared inside at us. He pushed his glasses up on his sweaty nose, his face redder than usual. He was yelling something, but I couldn't make it out. Then I saw the flame in the field across the road. It billowed bright orange with charcoal-y blossoms, swelling up, then bearing down, like it was panting for breath.

Mrs. Bonaventure opened the back door and grabbed her baby girl. Mom picked up the Bonaventure boy instead of me. James grabbed my hand as he climbed out the rear window, but I slipped free. The station wagon stood with all its doors open.

"Hurry up, before the gas tank explodes," Mom shouted but I couldn't budge. I watched as flames skipped among the haystacks and tents of smoke began to rise. The fire spread swiftly, gathering its own wind. Mr. Bonaventure seemed far away down the shiny tar road, running back the way we'd come. The babies' shrieking mounted to a siren's pitch that drilled inside my temples so loud that I couldn't think. The air inside the car was scorching, packed so tight that I could hardly breathe. A baby bottle in the seat pocket began to bloat and blister.

Mom screamed, but I was terrified that leaving the car meant diving into the mouth of a furnace. I had just turned ten in July, gotten a cake with carousel horses and pants with a candy-striped circus tent sewn on one leg. I was a big girl now. *Mommy!* I called or thought I had. But there was no sound.

I looked down at my hands, but they seemed far away, unattached to me. I watched as they gripped the rear door, then felt myself vault from the car. When my feet hit the bubbling tar road, my white tennis shoes sank into it. I tried to steady myself on the side panel of the station wagon, but it singed my hand, so I jerked it back. The panel was not wood, as

Afterheat
I had thought, but painted metal, which had begun to pucker. I ran toward Mom, my shoes sucking into the soft tar. The strip of road softened into black puddles that fused with my shoe soles. It felt impossible, like dream-running, where you raced as hard as you could, but got nowhere. My mother was only a few yards away, but I couldn't catch up.

    A searing wind buffeted my body, resculpting me, the contours melting away. I heard the flame's voice—ah aha ah aha—and saw my own flesh rolling in wet, pink slabs down my legs, filling my shoes with water. Inside my legs, blood clusters dotted the remaining flesh. My cousins always vied with each other to hold me in their laps, so precious, they said, in my bathing suit, my skin brown as a berry, though berries were not brown. Gazing up into the steep wall of flame made my eyes ache, but I could not look away. I breathed deep but couldn't get enough air. I was suffocating, inhaling dry fingers of flame.

    I crossed the sticky road and lay down in the brittle ditch grass. Both fields had caught fire. The crackling voice of the blaze overcame the high trilling of the locusts as it spread. It waved and spouted, dwarfing the oaks and poplars. Taller than the new water tower, wider than the hot air balloon I'd seen at the fair, though the flames wavered and shape-shifted like the balloon. It was bigger than anything I'd seen before and more magnificent. When I closed my eyes, the fire's afterimage shot flares of indigo and green behind my lids. I kept them closed. I wanted to rest. I wanted to sleep.

Suddenly, a hand grasped my right arm and jerked me roughly to my feet. The whites of James' eyes showed all around.

"Follow me," he said, and I did, alongside the fire, then away from it to where trees and barns blocked the heat. We found a farmhouse with a pick-up truck in the driveway. Mom wandered dazed in the front yard, a baby thrashing on her hip. I could see inside James' back, the fat and stringy pools of capillaries. The Bonaventures huddled with their baby girl in the surface roots of a giant oak.

In the distance, I heard car engines starting up and a woman's voice calling her dogs with increasing urgency, "Here, Ginger. Here, Paco. Ginger, Paco, Here, boys. Here!" A black farmer in overalls ran helter-skelter from his field behind the house carrying a long-handled hoe. He was so old that his hair was completely white and his eyes drained of pigment into a pale blue. "My Lord," he declared and pitched his hoe

Afterheat

into the grass. "The world is ending in fire."

He unlatched the gate of his truck and we all scrambled up into it. He had such a kind face that I thought maybe he was one of God's soldiers and this was how you got to heaven—carted up in the back of an old pick-up truck.

On the way to the hospital, I tried to raise my legs in the air to cool them down, but the wind opened my nerves. I dropped my legs and crawled across the bed of the truck to Mom. "Don't touch," she warned me sharply, holding up her palms, and I saw that her skin had melted, too.

Mrs. Bonaventure cried quietly and Mr. Bonaventure held his chest trying to catch his breath. James sat hunched over with his head on his drawn-up knees, shaking. The babies' howling told how I felt on the inside, but I was a big girl now, so I did not cry.

The waiting room was cool, though my legs stuck to the vinyl seats. When they lifted me, skin ripped from my thighs. They lay me on white sheets and nurses slid smooth scissors under my swimsuit, removing it in strips. Someone pulled off my shoes as something sharp and cold pushed into my arm. A moment later, I felt a rush of happiness as I drifted up and up.

Looking down, I saw the nurses wrapping and wrapping me with gauze until I was as fat as a mummy. They lifted me onto a stretcher and rolled me down the hospital corridors and into the parking lot. The Bonaventures were mummies, too, the babies quiet as they loaded them into an ambulance. I heard someone say Cincinnati. But Mom, James, and I rode in a different ambulance, home to Vance.

When doctors wheeled our stretchers down the halls of the Vance Hospital, Granny and Aunt Berry Mae rushed toward us, their hands in front of their faces.

Sometime later, the next day or the next, a hand appeared in front of me, setting a stuffed kitten on the nightstand. "His name is Socrates," Dad said. "He's traveled all the way from Texas." The kitten had bright yellow fur like a newborn chick and wore a mortarboard cap with a tassel. A tiny diploma hung from a satin string around its neck. Dad told me that Socrates was very smart and could answer any question I asked.

I tried to reach through the bars of the hospital bed, but the nurse spoke. "Can't touch, honey," she said. "The little toy is not sterile."

Afterheat

I wanted to tell Dad to make sure my cat, Kilroy, was okay, and ask him to please take a dollar to school to buy my flutaphone so I could learn scales. I was sure I'd missed school the day after Labor Day. In fifth grade, you learned scales on the flutaphone, and then in the sixth, you picked your instrument. I wanted to explain all of this to him, but I couldn't keep my eyes open long enough to focus on his face.

On the other side of the room, Dad murmured about a present he'd brought for James, something that spun on the floor like a top. Gyroscope, he was saying, angular momentum, defies gravity.

The nurses came and shot medicine into me with needles so often that I lost count of the days and nights. Mornings, the loud nurse came who ate from Mom's tray. "I'm partial to custard," she'd say, or "I was raised on pigs-in-a-blanket."

The television played day and night. I woke to static that whispered to me in patterns like crisscrosses, bridges, tunnels inside cities made of men's thighs and brave lungs and careless manners. Thumbnails paved the sidewalks and tongues corrugated the tile roofs. Dogs ran the streets with flowers in their fur.

Seven to three, three to eleven, eleven to

seven, marked the nurses' shifts. The morning nurse combed my hair straight up, and tied it into a ponytail on top of my head. The tight rubber band tugged at the roots as she sponged my face, talking nonstop in a voice like a light snapped on in the middle of the night. Her name, Bernadine, made me think of salted lemons. She tended to me in my crib near the door, to James in his low, rolling bed along the wall, and to Mom in her crank-up bed by the window.

At three in the afternoon, Mrs. Richardson arrived in her high, starched hat. She hummed to herself as she looked us over as though we were a pitiful bunch. Every hour I had to drink a glass of half orange juice half salt, for dehydration. Mrs. Richardson held the elbow straw so I could draw up the dense liquid while lying down. "Four more swallows," she encouraged me. Her fingertips were square and chapped, her nails thick with lengthwise ridges. "That's a good girl," she said.

One evening, as the women who wore soft shoes and hairnets rolled the dinner cart down the hall, I thought about how the metal domes rattled gently on the plates, a bell-like sound like the little glasses of sweet wine that clattered inside the communion tray at the Baptist church. Someone whisked through

Afterheat

the door and crossed the room with a tray for Mom. I caught the scent of something yeasty, rolls, maybe, and felt a sharp pang in my belly. I heard a clink as Mom lifted the dome, cursed under her breath, then another clink as she replaced it.

"Not hungry," Mom said to Mrs. Richardson, who hummed as she removed the tray. I heard the rasp of a match head against the sandpaper strip. When the fragrant blue smoke from the Lucky Strikes drifted past, I breathed it in.

"Fifty-fifty," I heard Mrs. Richardson whisper to the night nurse. A fifty-fifty chance. The little girl, Ruby, had third-degree burns over fifty percent of her body, she said. The Bonaventure children had been released from the hospital because they'd been burned only one square inch, the boy on his scalp, the girl on her arm. The mothers' bodies had shielded them from the heat. She said that the newspaper reported that Mr. Bonaventure had picked little Ruby up and carried her to safety. Mrs. Richardson seemed to believe that the story was true.

At eleven o'clock, the night nurse, who had glossy black hair and vivid red lips, sat in a chair and thumbed through magazines under a reading light.

One evening, the doctor arrived with two assistants who began slicing through the thick gauze around my arms and legs with blunt-nosed scissors. As they peeled off the layers, a scent like baking bread and ammonia wafted up as the cool hospital air settled onto my limbs. Blisters clumped down the right side of my arms and legs, plump and purple as plums.

"Turn on your left side, please," the doctor said.

As I shifted, Dad entered the room, followed by a man carrying a camera and tripod. Mrs. Richardson stopped mid-hum. As the man set up his camera, the doctor assembled his tray: various clamps, a basin, an enormous syringe. I thought the needle would hurt, but I didn't feel it go in, just a release of pressure as he proceeded to drain the big purple blisters on my arms and legs, drawing the fluid up though the needle. The photographer began shooting pictures.

"Why don't you just publish them on the front page of the damn *Sentinel*!" Mom shouted, drawing her thin cotton blanket over her breasts.

Dad moved to her bedside, and took one of her hands in both of his, as though proposing marriage. "We'll be glad to have these later on."

"You might be glad," Mom said. "I never want

Afterheat
to see them."

The photographer paused. Dad said quietly, "It's okay. Go on."

The draining relieved the pressure, but heat from the camera's flash nudged me as I lay naked on the starched white sheets. It was a gratuitous heat, like running over a dead animal on the road. More than once, I'd retrieved my own lifeless kittens from the road, their bodies deflated and light. Lying in the hospital bed, I felt flattened like those kittens, scruffy and twisted. If I died, maybe they would wrap me in flannel like I'd wrapped them, and I could huddle with them underground.

The doctor filled the basin with serum from my blisters and the assistant sprayed me with a white mist from an aerosol can. The camera kept on flashing. I imagined myself under the lens, half-skinned, hair raked back from my scorched neck, face sagging from exhaustion and constant sleep.

After the photographer finished, Mrs. Richardson lifted the bars of my crib and locked them in place. The photographer loaded another roll and began photographing Mom. I could see her through the bars, pressing a tissue to her face, her furious eyes. She wore nylon underwear cut out at the hip where the fire had seared through her swimsuit.

James was next curled toward the wall in his trundle bed. When the camera's bulb popped, his back brightened, like it was draped in strips of raw bacon. I thought about how white James' back had been as we swam around Chalk Lake that summer, churning through warm shallows spiked with frigid columns of deeper water. We hunted hot spots as well as cold spots, dog-paddling in circles in the green water. "Over here!" We called to each other. "No, here!"

Chalk Lake flooded before they'd finished clearing out the bottom, leaving the remains of the old farmstead. When Dad navigated our rowboat around slick black treetops that fingered above the surface, James sometimes managed to touch them, then rub the slime down my arm. "You've been marked by the Swamp Witch," he'd say ominously. "Beware." Divers brought up dripping trophies of chimney bricks and rusted lanterns. We swam until our hands and feet wrinkled and Mom ordered us out of the water. We climbed the mossy ladder and lay shivering on warm planks of the dock, the sun bleaching our hair the color of straw.

Lying in the crib, I remembered with perfect clarity the salt crystals on the hexagonal Cheese-

Afterheat

Nips. Starving, James and I sandwiched warm M&Ms, popped them so chocolate oozed between the little crackers, then gobbled them down. Dad strutted around the dock in bathing trunks, dispensing bottles of Dr. Pepper. He cracked beers for himself, tipping the can back, silhouetted in the sun. Dad was proud of his posture, stomach in, his chest pushed out. Fragrant with Coppertone, Mom sprang expertly from the diving board in her gold swimsuit. Her body arced high and distant, etched against the clear summer sky.

After the assistant and the photographer left, I heard the doctor explaining an operation to my Dad. He would shear the skin off my hips with a little machine and lay it in patches across the open places. There was more than one way to skin a cat, Dad always said, and I'd worried that he meant our cat, Kilroy. After all, he and Uncle Bud had castrated our horse, Sugarfoot, right in the field. I'd raced toward the frantic, neighing horse, but Dad had demanded that I stay back. I'd seen the knives, though, and the tray of blood.

"You're going to be all right," Dad said, after the doctor left, but his words did not comfort me. I wished I was not naked in the same room with my father; I wished Mom would talk.

CD Collins

At night, orderlies and janitors walked past the door, interrupting the bar of light beneath the door from the nurses' station, which was always lit. I could make out the outline of Socrates on the bed stand. I longed to hold him, stroke his fur. I'd named my real cat Kilroy, after a character Dad drew for us, a horizontal line for the wall, two eyes peering over a long nose, and fingers clamped on the line. He explained that American GIs left the sign as if to say—I was here, but you didn't catch me. It was a family joke, Kilroy turning over the food bag, scattering kibbles across the kitchen floor, Kilroy sharpening his claws on the arms of the couch, leaving his mark like the soldiers, "Kilroy was here."

Each night, Dad arrived at the hospital by six o'clock. He came straight from work at the Lexington Army Depot still dressed in his navy blue suit and white shirt, ties with rich, shiny colors like foil Christmas wrapping. His presence was cool like the air conditioning; it seeped into the sheets and chilled the bed's metal railing.

There was something wrong between my parents. I thought it had something to do with Dad hating Carl Bonaventure and here we had gone off to Red River with them. A wrong word from Dad, a

Afterheat

lightning look between Mom and a man, there could be trouble. "Can't you see your father's blitzed?" Mom would accuse me, as though my ignorance meant that I was on his side. Now, there was a quiet kind of trouble in the hospital room that made my feet squirm.

The night nurse told Mom that Mr. Bonaventure had fallen while sleepwalking in the Cincinnati hospital, tearing open skin that was just beginning to heal. "He said he'd been dreaming of running," the nurse said. "He woke up on the floor."

I pictured him sprawled there. Mr. Ladies' Man. Mr. Hollywood. Husbands suspected their wives were secretly in love with Mr. Bonaventure. Women laughed too much when he was around. Once, when Mom and I shopped for school clothes in Lexington, Mr. Bonaventure met us at the Saratoga restaurant. Mom said I could order anything I wanted, but when the hot fudge sundae arrived, I felt queasy. While they talked, I stirred the sundae into a muddy pool in the stainless steel dish. Mr. Bonaventure's knobby arms took up half the table as he spoke to Mom in a hushed voice, all tall and ruddy-skinned with lots of dark, curly hair and strange, heated-up blue eyes. I didn't understand why all those features put together were supposed to add up to handsome. They talked for a long time with gin and tonics between them on the table in the middle of the day. They said "he" and "she" instead of Claytis and Rose, like their names were curse words.

Dad called Carl Bonaventure "Diamond Dick" because of the way he'd gotten rich by building identical houses like on a Monopoly board. It took Dad twice as long to build a house, but he intended them to last forever. He always left a shade tree in the front yard and deep, rich earth for a garden. One day, Dad would quit his government job to go into construction for good.

One shot of morphine in the morning, one at night. Morphine made me float and laugh, especially the big shots, like for surgery yesterday when they came for me, dressed in green gowns and masks and guiding a thick, narrow stretcher. After the needle, I willingly rolled over onto the delicious green sheets, gazing into eyes above the masks, luxuriating at the touch of their capable hands. I thought maybe this feeling was like what liquor did for my dad. I wanted it too, that pillowy comfort. "Here we go!" I exclaimed, laughing, passing by the nurses' station. They waved and one of them said they'd see me in no time.

But in the operating room, it took them too

Afterheat

long to get the needle in, and the anesthesiologist complained, "Vein collapse." He jabbed at my wrists while my hands wriggled inside their straps. They strapped a mask over my face and I spun into orbit, straddling a shiny silver rocket, fireworks bursting in my path.

In ether sleep there are no dreams, just a day dropped out. I awoke in the darkened recovery room bundled in a thick cast from waist to chin, a fresh stinging on my left hip where they'd skimmed off skin. Ether sickness was like no other sickness I had known, the merciless nausea and weakness rolling through me. I leaned over the steel crescent, the nurse steadying my forehead. How could I be vomiting when I'd eaten only ice? Yet, I heaved uncontrollably.

"You have to be still, now," the nurse said, helping me back on to the cot. "Absolutely still, so the grafts can take."

Then I was back in Room 217, lying on my stomach, my right arm outstretched onto a board, an IV taped to one ankle. The needle knocked against my anklebone, bruising me. I managed to kick it out before submerging in sleep, which pulled at me like an undercurrent tugs down an exhausted swimmer.

CD Collins

I woke suddenly in my hospital bed, a terrible heat expanding behind my knees, inside my elbows. It rose from my neck and throat as an angry pain coiled inside my joints like red-hot metal springs. The shot had worn off. I felt the poke of the needle in my ankle again. My hip, raw beneath the gauze, pulsed so vividly it rose from my body like a sound, like children singing. The air conditioner clicked, then wound down. The night nurse was not in the room; she must have gone to the cafeteria. I could hear James' even breathing, Mom changing positions. I wanted to climb out. Out.

When the night nurse returned, I pretended to sleep. She closed the door quietly, stood for a moment in darkness, then settled into her chair. When I heard pages turning, I opened my eyes. The small, clamp-on light illuminated her pale skin beneath the nurse's cap. I didn't quite remember her name, just that it began with a G. Gwen. No, maybe a J, Janey, June. I wondered if she still thought that our chances were better than fifty-fifty. I strained to see the pages of the magazine as she turned them: desserts made of bright cubes of Jell-O, women showing off brilliant lipsticks, sailboats with smiling people dressed in white. If the nurse moved her chair next to my bed, we could look at the magazine together. I could touch her shining

Afterheat

hair, except it was not sterile.

My heart sped up and sweat formed on my scalp. Underneath the cast, the X of good flesh itched, where my bathing straps had been. If someone could touch me there, if someone could hold me, but there was not enough skin. The thumping of my own heartbeat knocked in my ears, alive, alive, it seemed to say. The body is a trap. It could be caught, set on fire, stolen through a window.

The nurse closed the magazine, checked her watch, fished a thick paperback out of her bag, and settled in reading again. I breathed slow and deep the way the people in the green surgical scrubs taught me. The nurse looked like an actress under a spotlight. Jackie, that was it! Jackie's hair was almost black, a brunette. People called James and me fair, which meant blond and light-skinned. Fair-complexioned. Caucasians were either fair or dark-complexioned like Frankie Gray, or they could be redheads like the Garret twins.

Four weeks inside the body cast was all. Then they would cut it off; then they would see. The flutaphones came in metallic colors; I wanted a bronze one, and a chart to learn scales. My hip would not always howl like this. I would look at magazine pictures with Jackie. As I breathed, I felt silence gathering inside me, mysterious and unknowable, the way a purr vibrated inside the blood of a cat.

Dad arrived at the hospital one morning in November wearing khakis and a tangerine-colored Orlon shirt. He'd brought a transistor radio and tuned it to WVKY. The radio played great, but was tiny and green like a mint.

"Let's listen for your names," he said. First, there was a show called *MysteryVoice*, when local people spoke in a distorted voice and told a riddle about themselves. The host chose numbers from the phone book, adding a dollar each time someone missed, until finally some smart person guessed right and hit the jackpot. On *Hospital Highlights*, the host read the names of everyone in the hospital and reported their condition—critical, stable, fair, or good. When they listed James and me as critical, Dad shook a fist at the radio. "Not true!" he exclaimed with a smile. "We're all doing fine!"

Today, Mom was listed as fair. They'd changed her condition because the doctors had found skin islands forming in the burned areas on her legs, arms, and neck; they were ninety percent sure she wouldn't

Afterheat

need skin grafts. The doctor said that Mom's skin had been tougher, because she was an adult. The islands rose from the seared rawness of her flesh, pink and new, the size of babies' fingertips.

The radio host announced one birth, John Raymond, weighing eight pounds, two ounces, a son born to Raymond and Polly Hester.

"All this town needs is another Hester," Mom said, and Dad joked that they needed the Hesters to fill up the jails.

"Johnny Hester is cross-eyed," James said. His legs had been protected by his long pants, but his back had burned deeply because he was fair-skinned. The doctors worried about his grafts not taking right, so Dad had helped Dr. Adams design a brace that hiked James' right arm to his shoulder level to keep it from fusing to his body.

"Close the door, Junior," Mom said. "Mrs. Winn is driving me crazy." Across the hall, an elderly patient with gangrene feet cried out day and night.

Mom calling Dad "Junior" was a good sign. She called him Claytis when she was accusing him of something. There were so many men named Junior in our extended family that they had to be distinguished by their last names. Mom and Aunt Phyllis complained about Dad and Uncle Bud drinking while sipping martinis on the back porch. Uncle Earl got sloppy, they said. Uncle Bud got reckless. Junior Anderson got happy. Junior Chambers got mean.

After Dad left, Bernadine came into the room and started getting me ready for my bath. She brushed my hair into its topknot, while James tossed spitwads at me from across the room with his good hand. His goal was to land an egg, made from tissue and saliva, in the birds' nest on the top of my head.

"Stop it, punk," I complained, dodging.

Bernadine ran warm water into a pink, rubber basin. Mom said all she wanted was to sink into a tub of warm water, a real bath. I wanted one, too, a bubble bath, the soft pile of a towel, rose-scented lotion. Bernadine handed me a toothbrush topped with peppermint paste. I brushed and spit into a cup.

While Bernadine soaped and scrubbed my unburned parts, she told my Mom the news.

"Well, apparently the little Starr girl, Wendy, got an invitation to a party out on the lake," Bernadine said, talking over the top of my head. "You know the Carmichael place, big old mansion up on the cliff where they used to have the fireworks before the drive-in opened."

Afterheat

Mom said that she knew the place.

"Well, the son decided he'd throw a shindig," Bernadine continued. "His parents can't do a thing with him. Child is eighteen and still needs a babysitter. His mother and daddy were off gallivanting God-knows-where. Little Starr girl's never going to be invited to cotillion, if you know what I mean, so I guess she jumped at the chance to hobnob with the country-club set. My daughter, Candace, was there, and said Wendy arrived with her hair all teased up into a French Twist, dressed in a pink satin shift with a chartreuse netting and pair of hot pink heels if you can picture all that."

"Six inch spikes, no doubt," Mom murmured from her cranked-up bed by the window.

"Tallest pair she could get her hands on, I'd say," Bernadine replied. "Candace said Wendy's dress was so tight you could see everything she had."

I glanced over at Mom to check her expression but she had turned to the window. She stared out all day sometimes, without a word, drawing slow and deep on her Lucky Strikes.

"Every teenager in town was there," Bernadine went on. "City school, county school, doctors' kids, preachers' kids, you name it, dancing all humped up like they do now. They said the music was so loud it rattled the windows in Sharpsburg. That kind of volume, they'll be half deaf by the time they're thirty, but of course wild horses wouldn't stop them. Girls were hollering for help from the cedar grove. I'll bet our nursery'll be plum full next spring with the spawn from that one party."

Bernadine finished sponging me off, pulled a sterilized towel from a paper package and began patting my good skin. "So," she said, raising an eyebrow, "Candace spots the Starr girl headed to the cedars with one of the Braxton twins, the boy whispering into Wendy's hair. And so, well, at least he had the manners to drive her home."

Bernadine paused for effect. "Evidently, Wendy was the one to find her mother at dawn at the bottom of that big long staircase. Of course, Marbury's people hurried over from Virginia wanting to know what had happened to their baby. The doctors really can't do anything for her, but she's in a private room down on the first floor, paralyzed from the eyes down and can't utter a solitary word."

"Pushed," Mom said, hunting around in her Whitman sampler for a caramel.

"Sooo..." Bernadine drew the word out like she was real satisfied with what she was about to say.

Afterheat

"Dallas was the only witness and he was laying up in the bed passed out. You'd think he would have heard the commotion. Either he was stone-deaf drunk or he is as lazy as everyone says."

Bernadine rinsed the soapy basins and put them away. "I hate to think what's going to happen to that child without her mama. Mmmm, mmm…" she hummed, which translated to, "How terrible." But even I knew Bernadine lived for scandal.

For two days, we heard Marbury's people from over in Virginia rustling around the hallways speaking in their peculiar accents, but nobody laid eyes on either Wendy or Dallas. One morning when she came in for her shift, Bernadine told Mom that Marbury was gone, lifted to a better life with her eyes wide open.

No one talked directly to James and me about what was happening to our bodies. We learned by eavesdropping, listening to the radio, reading the expressions on Dr. Adams' face when he examined us. The doctor waved the disinfectant aerosol can in the air above me. The cool spray sifted down, smelling of pine and baby powder. He prodded the leathery pieces that had cracked into jigsaw shapes covering my right side from my neck to my feet. "Axillary, peripherals," he said, pointing to me. "The arm. The leg."

They used a full can of aerosol on us every day. James collected the teal-colored caps, which were engraved with a rearing unicorn, lining them up along the windowsill.

Despite the grafts, my legs had bent double, heels at my buttocks. I climbed over the bars and scampered along the floor like a monkey. The nurses scolded me and lifted me back into the crib. I crouched on my mattress, watching skaters and dancers on TV.

The hospital didn't usually allow visitors, especially kids. But they let my friend Jen bring me schoolbooks and homework assignments. Mrs. Richardson draped the crib with a sheet to hide my body.

Jen stood awkwardly beside my bed telling me about school. "You'll get to learn Spanish when you get back," she said. "We do a half hour every day after lunch." Jen had won the spelling bee with the word "adiabatic," which meant keeping something steadily hot or cold like in a Thermos bottle.

"Do you think you can get caught up?" Jen asked. "If you pass, we can be in seventh grade together."

I told her I thought I could, but the pile of heavy

Afterheat

books on my bed stand seemed foreign, and even Jen seemed unfamiliar and out of place in her red wool jumper and knee socks. How could I explain to her about the beautiful unicorn caps and James' secret ice runs down the hallway the night before our operations. I wanted to tell her about the masked people who came in fast as kidnappers and how hilarious the world seemed after my shots, that I welcomed the needle that turned my vision silky and cool.

"Thanks for coming" was all I could think of to say, but it came out too soft, so I had to say it again.

Jen lifted the science book to show me what chapter we were on, but the heavy text tumbled from her hands and tore down the sheet, so that she saw the thick cast, arms, my whole body. "Ah!" she gasped, her hands covering her mouth. After she left, I made faces in the hand mirror on my bedside table, squinting until I looked like a monster.

In third grade, Jen and I had laid our heads on our desks while Mrs. Oldham read, the warm musk of mown hay drifting past us into the echoing hallway. While we listened, I marveled at Jen's hair, which gleamed the deep red of a sorrel horse. Up close, I could see the layers of autumn-colored crystals inside her irises. Jen was the smartest girl in class, which counted for a lot in third grade, and she had picked me as her best friend. She even invited me to Vacation Bible School in the First Baptist Church downtown, where we pasted uncooked macaroni and kidney beans onto cardboard in the shape of a cross, then spray-painted it gold. We read from a book with pictures of attractive, dark-skinned men who wore flowing housecoats and were known as the Apostles. We sat together on the hard church benches and sang:

I was sinking deep in sin far from the peaceful shore.
Very deeply stained within, sinking to rise no more.

I knew there was something I was supposed to believe, something about Jesus walking across the sea barefoot, salvation flowing from his upturned palms. Jen displayed generosity the way they taught us at church. She brought me homemade custard in a jar, and handed me sheets of paper when I ran out. Jesus had died for me, they told me in Sunday school, for Ruby Clay Chambers. Nothing was as precious as his mortal wounds.

Mom was moved to a private room down the hall. Room 217 felt empty now, with just James and me. I had trouble sleeping, so I took to watching Jackie, the

Afterheat

night nurse. I calmed myself inside the confinement of my cast, contracting and relaxing my muscles, so cool air could filter in. Controlling the atmosphere inside the heavy plaster generated a velvety pleasure. I thought about riding on sailboats like the ones in the magazine, gliding frictionless over the turquoise water, beneath wind-packed sails.

Once, while Jackie was on break, I pulled the heavy sheets between my legs, experimentally, and moved rhythmically against them. Images fluttered through my mind. I saw myself on the wooden dock at Chalk Lake standing next to God. Below, people wailed and drowned, imploring as the water surged and crested. I could feel the wind's force on my chest, which was bare and brave, shining. I wore a red velvet cape draped around my shoulders, tied at my neck with little silk ropes. Everyone on earth bobbed in the water and I was telling God whom to save. I pointed to Mom, who was plucked up by a silvery hand that reached down from the sky. Then Jen, Dad, James, and the Garret twins, Jim and John. All of them were hauled up, dripping and grateful. Jim and John were red-headed and identical, the cutest kids in town. I pressed against the sheets, faster, slower, faster. Black and red fragments shifted behind my closed eyelids as tension discharged from my body in jumpy waves. I sweated inside my cast, amazed by my discovery.

James turned restlessly in his sleep. As the flush subsided, I shivered, and drew my imaginary cape around my shoulders. With the red cape, I became noble, brimming with invincible love. I would save everyone on the Day of Judgment. My family, private loves, my sad mother, Pearl.

With Mom staying down the hall, James and I could make more noise, shouting along to the 45s on the hi-fi Dad brought for us: "Tower of Strength" by Gene McDaniels, who is miserable because he doesn't have the guts to leave his girlfriend, whom he hates; Floyd Cramer playing "Last Date" with the saddest, most romantic fingers on earth.

"Let's go, little girl," Bernadine said to me one morning as she locked the rubber wheels in place with the toe of one of her white shoes. She helped me into the chair. We rode the elevator down to the therapy room, where Dr. Adams and a couple of assistants hoisted me face down onto a narrow bed.

First, they sawed the cast down the middle of my back, then before I had time to be afraid, turned me over and ripped through the front, buzzing just below my chin, all the way down to my waist. When they

Afterheat

pried apart the halves, I felt like a chick pecked out of its shell, all shaky and free. Underneath the plaster, my unburned parts looked dull and shrunken.

Back in the room, Bernadine scrubbed me until I glowed pink, emptying basin after basin of soapy gray water. As a reward for getting my cast off, Bernadine draped my wheelchair and pushed us down to the cafeteria. James trotted behind, his right arm hiked up on its big steel arm brace. We ordered up strawberry milkshakes and drank them in the dayroom with windows all around. Outside, the bare tree limbs cast precise shadows onto the brick patio.

According to the nurses, James and I were getting rowdy. We rubbed the thermometer tip on the sheets till the mercury went to 110 degrees or stashed it in the ice bucket till it dropped to the temperature of a dead man. We stole ketchup packets from the dinner trays and squeezed clotted lines across our necks. When Mrs. Richardson returned from dinner, she found us frozen into crazy positions.

"Oh, they've died," she said, crossing her arms. "What a shame."

One evening, Jackie traded her shift with Mrs. Richardson and we begged her to take us to our mother's room for a surprise visit. Mrs. Richardson always said no.

"I don't know about that," Jackie said. James and I stared at her in silence. She looked first to one, then the other. "Oh, all right, munchkins," she said, and dipped a comb in water to slick back James' rusty blond hair. I climbed into my wheelchair, waiting, while Jackie rigged up some hospital gowns to screen me. We raced down the hall, squealing, Jackie veering my chair back and forth, James running ahead pretending to knock invisible enemies with his unconquerable Superhand.

When Jackie knocked on Mom's door, a man in street clothes answered. Inside the room, Mom rose from the edge of bed and disappeared into the bathroom. "Come in," the man said, "I'm Clark," the man said. "And you two must be..." Mom emerged wearing an eggshell-colored nightgown that billowed behind her as she walked. The air hung with powder and moisture. She kissed our foreheads, but she didn't seem especially happy to see us. I breathed in the steam, imagining the pleasure of her bath. My mother whispered something to Jackie, who nodded. She whisked us back down the hall as fast as we'd come.

Dr. Adams consulted with some Lexington doctors to try to figure out what to do with me. The

Afterheat

scabs on my legs hinged open like flaps of buckskin. I blew air from my lips, prying up the jigsaw edges to inspect the raw flesh. During evening rounds, doctors and interns gathered around me as I lay naked in my crib. They wore lab coats and pointed with gloved fingers while they discussed intrinsics and contractures. I sounded like I was rolling up like a ball of rubber bands. The only solution was to sever the tendons at the back of my knees.

"Will my hair ever grow back on my legs?" I asked Dr. Adams.

"No, lucky girl," he answered, flipping through my chart. "You won't ever have to shave them."

"Okay, here we go. She's coming up out of shock," I heard a faraway voice say. I heard papers rustling and the air was thick. I thought that meant surprise, but I was disintegrating, an Alka-Seltzer in the ocean, fizzing out from the center.

When I woke again, I opened my eyes. Jackie sat near my bed with one of her hands resting on my pillow. I could feel my legs, long and flat against the sheet. Tentatively, I touched her hand with my fingers, and when she held it there, I clasped a hand over hers. Inebriated by the nutty, fruity scent of Jergen's lotion,

I nuzzled my cheeks into her warm palm. When she placed her other hand on my hair, my eyes spilled over. I held on fast.

After a week, they got me up to practice walking. After a few days, I was able to clomp all the way to the nursery, peg-legged like Chester on *Gunsmoke*, Bernadine at my elbow. We rested at the end of the hallway, peering through the glass at the new babies fidgeting in clear bins, their last names written in blue ink on signs at their feet: Fawns, boy. Overstreet, girl. They wiggled constantly, even in sleep, grabbing the air with their little wrinkly hands, their bluish fingernails already in need of a trim.

Everyone in the hospital was invited to the Christmas service in the little chapel, which was usually reserved for relatives of dying patients. James took his time dressing in his black slacks. He wanted to do it himself. Dad cut the right sleeve from James' dress shirt with a pair of sharp hospital scissors, so he could fit his brace through the hole. He handed it to him behind his privacy screen. After a long time, James appeared, red faced but fully dressed. Bernadine had buzzed his hair, so his big ears stuck out like Dumbo the elephant's.

I got to wear a cotton johnny tied in back, with

Afterheat

another on top of it, tied in front. The gowns hung in loose folds around me and I was relieved that only my head, hands, and feet showed. Bernadine pulled terrycloth slippers on my feet and I stood up, gripping the floor with the treads.

My legs were straight now, but I had to work to bend them at the knee. The sight of descending stairs made my stomach shake, but today I was going to walk to the Christmas service on my own. Bernadine walked alongside me down the short flight of stairs and past the gift shop. There were a dozen things to think about to keep myself from falling on my face. Lifting one foot, bending my knee, holding to the rail till my foot steadied on the next step down. The chapel was a square room with rows of padded metal-backed chairs, a wooden podium mounted with a wooden cross and fiery poinsettias placed at each corner. Bernadine stood behind a chair near the door, holding it in place while I slowly sat down. I had to concentrate on each movement, as though my body were a puppet, its strings operating one at a time.

Carmen Gray and Mom smoked cigarettes out in the hall, leaning against the wall and flicking their ashes into the big, sand-filled canister. Sitting there, I overheard Mom saying something about rubbers and thinking her skin might rip, but that she hadn't cared one bit. She wore a turquoise angora sweater and cream-colored straight-legged pants. "I'm sick to death of looking like some crazyhouse inmate."

James and Dad sat in the front row with Aunt Phyllis. The black-haired, green-eyed Goodpasters took up the entire second row. They were here visiting their brother, who'd gotten his arm caught in a corn thresher. The Winns sat behind them, their bones delicate, their silver-blond hair shining, even old Mrs. Winn, bowed and demure in her wheelchair, too drugged to complain.

When Reverend Colley took the podium, the room instantly hushed. Mrs. Colley arranged herself on the piano bench and began to play, the tone dark and flowing. "Let all mortal flesh keep silence," Reverend Colley sang, his rich tenor resonating inside my chest. After the first verse, the congregation joined in, and Mom slipped into the seat beside me. Her brittle alto, like a knife blade on whetstone, always hit the note dead on. At the end of the song, we sang amen till we ran out of wind, but Reverend Colley held the note, his eyes heavenward and shining.

I knew the outlandish story he was about to tell. For me, it blended together with the spruce tree

Afterheat

in front of the courthouse that glowed with heavy, old-fashioned bulbs and the way I felt proud when the high school band marched past in their royal blue uniforms. I loved the Christmas parade, the fantastical floats, the thrill I felt seeing snowflakes caught in the thick hair of the marching drummers. Standing on the street in the cold created an expectant longing, as though the lights on the spruce tree were drops of luminous candy, which could dissolve magically on my tongue and soothe the rankling in my belly. Today, listening to Reverend Colley sustain his blazing note, I believed it all again.

During the closing prayer, I remembered a Christmas Eve when I'd been wakened deep in the night by the sound of Mom's raised voice "…listened for your damn car after each icicle I hung on the tree," I heard Mom say. "You've been drinking with that bastard Joe Whitson…"; "wrapped presents all night…"; "all by myself…" A deep, muffled sound of apology, then Mom starting up again. The argument had confused me, because that evening we'd decorated our tree with cranberries on strings and new lights whose bulbs boiled water inside colored glass tubes. I listened to Mom's and Dad's voices, trying to untangle words that ran into and on top of each other like a demolition derby. I pulled my feet from the cold spot at the bottom of the bed and hugged my pillow. I hadn't known. I thought we'd had a grand time. I thought we'd had a party.

A few weeks before we were released from the hospital, a crop of boils buckled the good skin on my lower back and inner thighs. Boils clustered in my armpits so I couldn't rest my arms at my sides. Dr. Adams told me that every boil was worth five dollars because they were poison working its way out. Carbuncles clustered in my armpits like purple fox grapes, and ran down my arms like leprosy. The boils literally exploded and the relief was always better than the hot, tender pain.

After the hospital, my mother said there was no cure for me but the ocean, so with the money from our insurance settlement, Mom, James, and I flew to Hawaii. We didn't know at the time that she had no intention of going back.

We flew all around the islands on Aloha Airlines—Oahu, Maui, and the Big Island, Hawaii. Men hounded my mother without pause. Happy that she could still enthrall men, she let them come too

Afterheat

close. Once we had to flee through a back alley to our hotel, Mom's spike heels tapping the pavement like the hooves of a panicked doe. That whole evening, we hid in our hotel room with the lights out.

James and I bodysurfed in the glassy curls of the fifteen-foot waves that flung us onto black sand beaches and shot sea water into our ears and up our noses. James' legs were skinny and white, but untouched by burns. His back was fuchsia straitjacket, webbing his right arm, so he couldn't stroke overhead as he swam. The sea roiled our flesh, cleaning us inside and out. We ate tropical fruit, roast pig, and a purple pudding made from taro root. Poi, it was called; two-finger, three-finger, depending on the thickness of the paste. In the cool bungalows, the sound of waves rocked us to sleep.

We rented a house on a Maui cliff that overlooked the sea, but we had to leave because it was infested with square-nosed rats. We heard them scuttling and thumping around the kitchen, turning over groceries in the night. While we shopped in town, one of the natives told Mom that the woman who owned the house was harboring a Nazi. He was somewhere on the property, in the attic or nearby forest waiting for us to leave. The townspeople had put the rats there themselves to drive him away. Mom lay awake all that night. The next morning we called a taxi and told the man to drive us straight to the airport.

Back on the Big Island, Mom called Dad. We'd spent most of our money on a month's rent but had stayed less than a week. I stood in the alley around the corner from the public phone booth, eavesdropping. "What do you mean?" My mother said, her voice becoming agitated. "It's my money, too." Then, "They're your children, too. You can't do this."

We ended up staying at one of her suitors' houses, which was practically a palace, with a long swimming pool bordered by lemon trees. Mr. Ko'olau was a native Hawaiian with a gentle voice and good manners. He set up dancing classes for me and scuba lessons for James. I rolled my hips to the hula and agitated them wildly to guttural Tahitian chants. My body ached with stored-up energy; I craved motion.

The movement shook loose the stagnation of my sedentary year. I sweated off the stink of chemicals and shook until new muscle burned through the accumulated hospital fat. Mr. Ko'olau wanted to marry my mother, and I know she must have been tempted as she walked with him on the veranda and peered at the tropical birds through his binoculars.

One bright afternoon, a teenaged boy and I

Afterheat

were swept into the same crashing wave. We tumbled underwater, our limbs entwined. Both struggling to stand, he grinned at me, then dove back into the ocean. As he swam away, the sight of his glistening brown back and the rise of his buttocks in his tropical-patterned jams caused a vertigo that forced me to kneel in the swirling shallows. When I stood up, I looked down at my body in a green floral two-piece. Though scarred down my right side, I was strong and shimmering, smooth skin grown over the healed boils. Mom had been right. Hawaii was the cure.

"What if we lived here all the time?" I asked James the next morning at a breakfast café. I was having pancakes with papaya syrup. "It'd be great," he said. "I could eat pineapple and poi and go to college at the University of Hawaii."

James looked down at his plate. He'd come down with a case of swimmer's ear and went around with oily-looking cotton balls hanging out the sides of his head.

"I miss Flip," he said. "And Dad."

"Dad's a sumbitch," I said with authority, compressing "son of a bitch" the way Mom did.

"Take that back," James said, pointing his fork at me. "Now."

"Make me." I sprayed whipped cream onto my waffles and sawed into them. James knocked over my tower of whipped cream with his fork and glared at me. "You always take up for Dad, no matter how awful he gets."

It was true. Every time Mom tried to leave Dad, James would take to his bed, crying. I'd have to yank him up and half drag him into the idling car. Mom said he was tenderhearted.

We left the Big Island as abruptly as we'd left Maui. My mother packed us up one morning and Mr. Ko'olau sadly drove us to the airport. "A hui hou kakou," he said, arranging orchid leis around our necks and kissed us each goodbye. "Until we meet again."

Inside the plane, I closed my eyes and thought of the Hawaiian boy in the surf. I pictured him at a sock hop, dressed in flowered shirt and slacks, slowdancing with me in perfect rhythm. He'd fold his body around me, hands pressing into the small of my back. With my dance records in my suitcase, my skin browned, my hair bleached by the sun, and my newly lean physique, I gazed down from the porthole as the ocean disappeared.

After the hospital, I pushed against something

Afterheat

every day. I worked hard to make my legs limber again so I could drop into a chair without thinking, or chase James downstairs. In high school, I would join track, train as a lifeguard, carrying a lead weight on one hip while swimming the length of the pool. Running like mad, I would pass boys on the track and pick them off one by one. If I endured the wavering heat rising from asphalt tracks, if I kicked hard up from the bottoms of pools, I thought I might save someone. Then I would feel peace, for a moment, or an hour.

Happiness is an increase of power, so said Nietzsche. Happiness is the cessation of pain. I'd had so little power at the Saratoga restaurant, stirring my hot fudge sundae and feeling sick. After the accident, the newspaper said that Mr. Bonaventure had saved me, had reached his arms into the inferno and lifted me from the maw of death. But I had seen him run away that day and so had my mother, so I knew for sure that she knew about the mettle of her good-looking Mr. Bonaventure.

The underground gas lines had been laid quickly during the war, the unlined pipes unable to withstand high internal pressures such as those that built up that day beneath Indian Fields. Everyone said the burst pipeline left a crater like an A-bomb. The explosion was like an A-bomb inside our family and I knew nothing could ever be safe after that.

But I tried to make it safe. If I could learn about gas pipes and A-bombs, and how skin islands could grow on patches of raw flesh, maybe I could keep accidents from happening.

Later, when I read about Oppenheimer, I imagined that he must have been mesmerized, simultaneously hating and loving his creation, like the sun rising right in his face, changing everything. They said that the people who watched from ten miles away had expected the size and bright light and the wind. But they hadn't expected the heat.

The vaporization of a person is the conversion of the body into free molecules by the force of heat and light, a boiling into the air. In Hiroshima, this event recorded an impression on nearby walls, a kind of simple photograph such as those made by pinhole cameras fashioned from oatmeal boxes. Objects in the path absorbed some of the radiant light as they dematerialized. A concrete wall does not reveal subtle gradients of contour and light as would a segment of silver-impregnated celluloid or a sheet of light-sensitive paper. It is a shadowy image, yet a true photograph, that is, an image produced by the chemical action of light, including X, gamma, or cosmic rays. It is not a shadow, as has sometimes been assumed, because shadows characteristically disappear when the illuminated subject is removed.

Chapter 7
Hurricane

The red shutters against the Grays' house were the first thing I noticed when Mom steered our car down Mitchell Street. I'd turned eleven in Hawaii and now it was almost time to start school again. I'd missed the whole sixth grade, but the counselor tested me in the school cafeteria and decided to pass me anyway. James and I were now in the seventh grade. "Your Mom and Dad need a special kind of Florida vacation for just the two of them," Aunt Phyllis told me. James would stay with Grandpa Chambers out in Greenbriar, where our dog, Flip, lived now and the Grays would look after me.

When Mom pulled the Pontiac into the driveway, my stomach fluttered at the thought of the Grays' son, Frankie, his slender body and slow smile.

Afterheat

In the spare bedroom across the hall from Frankie's room, Mom smoothed the nubby chenille bedspread and raised the window blinds.

"See, you have a pretty tree outside your window," she said. "And a hi-fi. Look at all those 45s."

I parted the sheer curtains and peered up into the leaves. Gold leaked from the edges into the green centers. "Do you and Dad have to be gone a whole month? Won't that cost a lot?"

"We'll be back before you know it," Mom said and kissed the top of my head, something she never did. I pulled away awkwardly and opened my suitcase to retrieve the necklace made from kukui nuts and puka shells we'd bought at the shop near our hotel in Hawaii. I was proud to present such a grand gift to Carmen. "Let's give it to her, now," Mom said. She followed me down the hall to the kitchen where Carmen was making one of her jambalayas. Steam poured from a giant pot as Carmen shook in cayenne pepper. She was dressed all in orange: a sleeveless blouse and cotton skirt which seemed to pulsate against her smooth, dark Cajun skin.

"For me!" Carmen exclaimed when I handed it to her. She draped it around her neck, admiring it as I explained that the nuts were candlenuts and that

Hawaiians burned them for their oil. The necklace would also protect her.

"Honey, I could use some protection in this old town," Carmen said.

"Couldn't we all?" Mom said. She handed Carmen a bottle we'd brought along from the doctor, a blend of peanut oil, rosewater, glycerin, and lanolin. My scars had healed but were thick and uneven, marking my arms and legs like lava flow.

"Twice a day," Mom said. "Then she has to stretch her arms over her head, hold, then touch her toes." As she lifted her arms, the hem of Mom's dress rose above her white slip. "The doctors are trying to get more range of motion."

"I'll oil her up so slick no one can hold on to her," Carmen said, coming around the counter to squeeze me tight.

When Carmen said "slick," it sounded like "sleek." Sleek as glass, she exclaimed about roads in winter, sleek as a ribbon. Carmen's accent made words sound new. "Smort," she said, instead of "smart." She knew Frankie was smort if he would just buckle down. But it seemed like Frankie could never make sense of the numbers and letters in schoolbooks, no matter how hard he tried. Sixteen in the sixth grade, so far

Afterheat

behind all he wanted to do was drop out. This year, Carmen had finally let him quit, provided he got a job hotwalking horses at Keenland race track.

A few days after my parents left, we all gathered to watch TV—Buster in his Naugahyde recliner, Frankie stretched out on the braided rug. Carmen perched on the couch and brushed my hair while I sat cross-legged on the floor in front of her. She squeezed the oil concoction into one palm, whisked her hands together, and massaged deep into my arms. My scars were like a topographic map, thick ridges with less feeling than my natural skin, combined with shallow valleys as sensitive as lips. In the hospital, I'd gotten used to all kinds of procedures, but here in front of Frankie and Buster, I felt my face go red.

After the news, the weatherman traced the path of a hurricane headed straight up the Florida coast, toward Palm Beach. I jumped up from the floor and Carmen's hands flew off me. "That's where Mom and Dad are!" I said, pointing at the television. "Jupiter Hotel, it's right on the beach." The roof could peel off, exposing my parents like in a dollhouse. "We have to call!"

"They'll be fine," Carmen said, gently tugging

me back to my place between her legs. I sat back on the floor, my eyes riveted on the television. She worked coconut oil into my hair, braiding it into a single pigtail, then wound a rubber band around the end. "In New Orleans, we just boarded up our windows and played poker. You always know what a hurricane's going to do."

"If they're so predictable," Buster said, "why do they give them women's names?" He picked up a beer opener and punched two triangles in the top of a can of Black Label. Carmen allowed him two cans of beer per night.

"They're calling this one Nadine," Frankie drawled. He wore straight-legged jeans and a denim shirt with the sleeves cut out to show the twining muscles under his skin. His dark brown hair curled to a point on his forehead.

"Don't listen to them," Carmen said to me. "They're both silly. If there is a problem, your mother will call. I know that for sure."

"Okay," I said, trying to calm myself. "We've got the hotel's number."

"Yes, honey," Carmen said. "We do."

Carmen rubbed the oil in briskly, giving me a sensation of simultaneous pleasure and hurt. By the

Afterheat

time she finished, I prickled hot and shiny all over.

After dinner, I diagrammed sentences in my room while Frankie built model cars in his room across the hall. Frankie had all the best things in a boy—dark skin, full lips, a long, loose-jointed body. I'd seen him outside the pool hall smoking cigarettes when I rode through town with Mom. His good looks dazzled me, like those boys onscreen at the Trimble Theater whose lives descended into tragedy.

As I broke down reading problems into numerical equations, the vapors from Frankie's enamel paint crept under my door. I wondered what colors he was using, candy-apple red, maybe, or Bel-Air blue, James' favorites. Next, I opened my science book to the chapter on planets. We were supposed to draw diagrams that showed how we see the moon in its phases. According to Mrs. Ramsey, the phases occurred because different fractions of sunlight reflected from the moon to earth in its orbit. "It's not the earth's shadow on the moon. That's a lunar eclipse," she said. "Just close your eyes and picture the earth and moon, spinning and rotating, a big sister and little brother, circling the sun."

I loved Mrs. Ramsey's lessons, passionate, like a preacher. I even liked her strict rules and sarcastic humor. She wore her black hair combed straight back, red lipstick and fitted wool dresses. Every day before lunch, she would sit at her desk and meaningfully pull a tube of lotion from her desk drawer. As she lathered her hands, she'd call our rows. "Five…one…six…three." When we heard our number, we rushed to line up at the door.

I finished half of one diagram in my notebook. I could hear Frankie in the next room, whistling to himself. I turned to a new page in my notebook and drew ocean waves. Someday, I'd see the Atlantic Ocean, too. I would dive right in. According to Dad, Florida houses were built from sand and plaster with colored sea-glass stuck into the facades. They made hotels from blocks of something called coquina, cut from beach caves with a machete. The streets sparkled, he said, and every house had an orange tree in the backyard. I thought maybe we couldn't call the Jupiter Hotel because the Grays could not afford long distance. Even at home, when someone called long distance, no one made a sound. We could practically feel the money draining from our bank account till the receiver was returned to its cradle.

Getting off the bus at the Grays' house, I held on

Afterheat

to the rail and stepped carefully down the corrugated rubber steps into the October sun. I was never sure my knees would bend at the right time. I hung my school clothes in the closet and pulled on my soft red T-shirt and blue pants with the circus tent appliquéd to the right leg. The top button had worn off, so I fastened the waist with a safety pin. I'd gotten the pants for my birthday. I had decided to wear them until my parents came home safe.

Frankie knocked once, then opened the door.

"Hey, Ruby," he said. "You home early?"

"Bus lets me off first," I said, fooling with the buckle on my book satchel.

He walked in and closed the door. He seemed huge inside the room in his red-and-white checked cowboy shirt and tight jeans. He rolled his sleeves to his elbows, exposing his muscular forearms, and sorted through the 45s. When he knelt, we were the same height.

"Want me to show you 'The Twist'?" he said, sliding a record onto the ejector.

"Cool," I said, kicking my book satchel under the bed out of the way. I already knew "The Twist."

Frankie twirled the knob, the tone arm searched, and the record dropped onto the dusty turntable. The needle popped for a second on the vinyl before burrowing into the groove. "Come on baby, let's do the Twist," Frankie lip-synced.

Frankie swayed back and forth and moved his arms from side to side. He tried to catch my gaze but I wanted to concentrate on the rhythm and show him I knew how to do it right.

Halfway through the song, Frankie took off his loafers, then lay on my bed, his back to the wall. He patted the bed, inviting me. I hesitated, then crawled onto the bed beside him, my heart pounding. Up close, he smelled of leather and the sweet musk of horses.

He unwrapped a stick of chewing gum and tore off half for me, holding it high with one arm, beyond my grasp.

"Open," he said, softly.

I opened my mouth and he folded the gum, warm from his pocket, onto my tongue.

"See this," Frankie said, holding up his index and middle finger of his right hand. "When I make a V, you part your legs. Could you do that for me? It'll feel good."

The blinds cut the October sun into bars of gold across the chenille spread as Frankie pulled off my socks. He unfastened the safety pin and pulled down my pants, dropping them in a mound on the floor. "My daddy is sleepin', and Mama ain't around..." I lay quietly in my underwear and T-shirt, my scars exposed. Frankie was beautiful, so beautiful. Why had he picked me?

He gave me the sign with his fingers and slid his body over mine, still dressed, supporting himself on his elbows. He moved his hips in subtle rhythm to the song. I concentrated on a pearl button on Frankie's shirt, a kaleidoscope of gray and white. I thought of Chubby Checker with his round, smiling face and stretchy houndstooth suit, making everything look happy and easy. The song ended, and the tone arm searched again, the diamond needle circling through static.

The song played three times before we heard the crunch of Carmen Gray's shoes in the deep gravel. Frankie raised himself up without rushing. He must have known his mother's habits, how long it took her to climb the long drive and retrieve the mail from the box, check the last of the roses. I closed my eyes, heard Frankie close the door to my room, then the door to his own. I pulled my T-shirt back down, snatched up my pants, and yanked them on. What if Carmen found out, what if Frankie took off my underwear? After dinner that night, we watched the white swirl on TV that marked the progress of the hurricane. One of its arms hooked up into Palm Beach. I clasped a pillow to my chest and stared into the screen.

Buster sipped his beer and studied the hand-carved Chinese checkerboard set up on a collapsible TV table between him and Frankie.

"I bet your parents send us a postcard from one of those glass-bottomed boats," he said.

Carmen dished out slices of a butterscotch cream pie that she'd brought home from the factory, sliding the plates onto the Formica bar. Frankie drew out his pocketknife and cleaned his fingernails with the blade tip while he waited for Buster to make his move. The silver glare from the television glazed Frankie's eyes, so that I couldn't read his expression. I worked my fork through my slice of pie and let it dissolve in my mouth.

The next afternoon, Frankie didn't knock. He just came in and put on the 45. He set a cold Orange Nehi on my bureau. "Something for you," he said, uncapping the bottle. When he touched me, I thought of giant shapes, hollow letters, spelling out my mother's name. I saw myself filling the "P" with white concrete. In my imagination, the letter was taller than

Afterheat

me, so I used a stepladder to fill it in, one trowel at a time. I smoothed the top with the trowel's edge, and then made a mosaic of bits of colored glass and jack rocks on the wet surface. Before I reached the "r," I heard Carmen's steps in the gravel.

The Grays took me down to October Court Day, the weekend all the mountain people descended into Vance to barter—hound dogs and shotguns, antiques and sorghum molasses. We went to see Frankie riding bareback in a rodeo show in a grassy field over by the railroad track. Carmen had embroidered a hummingbird in bright colored threads on the front lapel of his denim jacket. I thought that if my Mom were here, she'd be flirting with Frankie with that wistful tone she reserved for good-looking men. Any woman rated lower on Mom's scale than any man.

I balanced on the top rung of the slat fence and watched Frankie mount the horse at the center of the dusty corral. The animal bucked and kicked, flailing its hooves and rolling its eyes back till the whites showed. I gripped the fence, transfixed by the spectacle of Frankie breaking his mount. The horse pawed the air desperately, but Frankie stuck to it like a barnacle to a ship. In the end, the horse's mouth foamed and its head drooped toward the ground.

One night, Buster and Carmen decided to go out dancing on a steamboat called *The Boonesboro Belle*, a Dixieland band would play on the deck while the boat churned up and down the Kentucky River. Buster fussed with his silver cufflinks and turquoise string tie while Carmen swished around the house in her flared green dress. Frankie had already left for Teen Rendezvous, a dance hall for kids over fifteen. He'd worn a sports jacket and polished his boots.

"Here, honey," Carmen said, taping Buster's sister's phone number to the wall beside the telephone. "Anything happens, you dial this number. Even if you just get scared."

Buster grabbed Carmen from behind and whirled her around. She shrieked, revealing the gap between her front teeth. Buster dipped her so low that her black hair swept the linoleum. "You're too old to cut the mustard, Mr. Gray," she teased, but he just laughed and dipped her down again.

After they drove off, I reared back in Buster's recliner and ate the ice cream and brownies Carmen had laid out for me. I watched Red Skelton sew his lips together with an invisible needle. Red Skelton lived in the city dump and could make one teabag last a whole

Afterheat

month by dipping it for two seconds each morning in a cup of hot water. His address was Number One Paradise Lane.

The Andy Williams Show came on next. At the end, he sang with his whole family as they perched on tall stools in matching V-necked sweaters. On the news, the weatherman pointed to the spiral of clouds over Florida. The winds had reached 110 miles per hour, he warned, as if we viewers could do something about it, and the storm was gaining strength. The broadcast showed palm trees bent so low that their crowns beat the pavement.

I couldn't stand to hear any more about the hurricane, so I switched off the television and tiptoed into Frankie's room. Our rooms were identical—a twin bed under the window, a pine bureau along the opposite wall, a tiny closet in the corner. Bottles of cologne and painted model cars were lined up along his bureau. I thought Frankie was the kind of boy I'd want to go steady with later on. I knew that he had plenty of girlfriends now, pretty ones with makeup and breasts.

I'd taken dancing lessons, though; tap, ballet, jazz. Maybe one night Frankie would ask me out dancing, then he'd be surprised. I opened the bottles on his bureau, one at a time, until I found the coffee scent that lingered in the air after he was gone. "Don't you feel it?" Frankie always asked me. I nodded yes, but it was a lie. I couldn't feel it, but I wanted to.

I couldn't tell how long I'd been asleep when I was awakened by a weight on my bed, a subtle rocking presence, like my cat jumping up to sleep beside me. I smelled cologne with a sour undertone of liquor and felt warm fingers loosening the buttons of my pajamas. Cool air skittered across my chest. Frankie leaned close, a forefinger pressed to his lips. "Shhh," he said, no louder than the breeze shivering beneath the window. In the darkness, Frankie removed my pajamas and climbed in beside me. His skin felt warm and his hands seemed to reach around my whole body, moving me this way and that, but quietly, like mime.

I thought of Red Skelton as he unbuttoned a pretend shirt and hung it lovingly on a hanger in his imaginary closet at Number One Paradise Lane. He'd pulled on his invisible pants, left leg, right leg, hoisting them above his waist and ripping them in half. He held them up with his fingers, gaping from side to side; he hadn't realized how threadbare they had become. The audiences seemed to love his slapstick humor, but I couldn't tell if they were real. Canned laughter it was

Afterheat

called, like those cans with compressed snakes inside. When you opened the lid, a cotton snake with wire insides sprang out.

I believed that if a boy wanted something from a girl, then she was bound to give it. His desire became her desire. In return, he cherished her. Frankie hovered like a shadow over me, then something bulky moving between my legs. I turned my face to the side, forming a cave of air beneath his chest. Tonight, he kept going. The friction made me see sparks like the ones that flew up from the electric whetstone in my grandfather's basement. "Don't look," Pa warned me. The brightness will burn your eyes to cinders. Frankie's breath heaved somewhere above my head, and I could feel the high-pitched rasp of the blade like it was buzzing down the roots of my teeth.

I'd seen the word for what we were doing scrawled on the side of the school with spray paint. If the Grays came home, Carmen would rush in, snap on the overhead light, and drive me out of the house. I'd be branded.

I thought of Andy Williams and his family on stools under the spotlight singing in harmony in their red V-necked sweaters. As Frankie moved faster, I felt a ripping sensation and clamped my eyes tight, reversing the red sweaters to a corrosive green. Andy Williams' silvery black skin resembled an X-ray. I could see inside the faces of his children to their teeth, their throats opened wide and the high notes came out clear and true. Andy Williams' teeth flickered white to silver to black.

I held still inside my mind. The more powerful the hurricane, the calmer the eye. I floated there with Mom and Dad in a clear sky, the aquamarine sea shimmering below. The eye was seven miles deep wrapped in a wall of sinewy clouds, circling around the way Frankie's arms encircled me now, holding me fast, his breathing charged, his heart rabbit-kicking. His torso waved in a slow, dense rhythm, then faster, then something warm.

"It's okay," Frankie whispered in my ear. "You're okay. You're my girl now."

The next evening, I tried to figure out math homework in my room, translating reading problems into numbers. If Mrs. Brown went to the store for a dozen oranges... In Florida, everyone planted orange trees in their backyard, so said my father. In Florida, all the houses were built of crushed shells and coral cut from sea caves with a machete. If Mrs. Brown walked

Afterheat

two blocks in five minutes, if the store was four blocks away… I wrote the number four like a little triangle flag, the number two with a looped base like a cursive capital Q. I made sure my margins were neat.

In the living room, Carmen and Buster laughed along with the television's laugh track. Canned laughter. Canned like tomatoes, or peanuts, or chewing tobacco. Working reading problems made my eyes ache, but I had to finish them. I had to be sure there were no mistakes. I had to make one hundred.

If Mrs. Brown lived in Florida, why did she walk to the store for oranges? If Frankie came into my room every afternoon, why didn't he look at me in the living room? If the hurricane weren't dangerous, why were they charting its path on television? I sharpened my pencil and wrote sevens with a little cross on the stem. In seven days, my parents would return from Florida, safe from the hurricane. They would drive down Mitchell Street and pull into the Grays' driveway to pick me up. I would hear the engine halt, then the heavy click of the car doors.

The dense cloud rose eight miles into the air above Hiroshima, drifted northwest, and then back again, raining upon the city, the inhabitants of which a half hour before had begun their work day under a clear sky. The rain was black and composed of water vapor, carbon, and ash, what remained of former trees, animals, wood, and people.

Chapter 8
Big As Life

That crisp, sycamore-scented morning, the bus driver, Mrs. Barrows, picked James and me up the same as always. Next, the Spencer boys; Becky Becraft, whose foot had gotten caught in my bicycle spokes; the Stockdale clan. I had dirt clod fights with all of them, and ridden in the backs of their parents' trucks to the Judy Drive-In. We swam naked in ponds and made failed fireworks from sand, match heads and flowers swung around and around in a bucket. We danced on the Spencers' back porch to "Wings of a Dove." We'd all ridden home early on that day last year when our handsome young president had been shot dead. Mrs. Barrows stopped at the tracks and levered the doors open to listen for the train. She closed the doors and the bus slowly trundled over the rails.

Afterheat

We picked up the McCormick boys, who'd all grown about a foot over the summer. Then the bus stopped in front of a brown-shingled house and a neatly dressed black girl boarded the bus. I had passed this house on my bicycle a thousand times, but had never seen this girl. When she got on, we all hushed as she walked down the aisle, her shoes making a soft sound on the hard rubber floor mat. I looked up at her but she was staring straight ahead. She picked a seat near the middle and held her book satchel with both hands on the lap of her starched periwinkle dress.

The bus made five more new stops that morning that silenced our first-day chatter—a tall, caramel-skinned boy with eyes pale as moonlight, a set of twins in matching sashed dresses. The new riders chose the wide empty seats. No one spoke to them, nor they to us. I didn't understand why I hadn't seen them ripping up and down the road on English racers but I knew why I hadn't seen them creating towering blue splashes we made as human cannonballs from the diving board at the city pool. The first day of my freshman year in high school was also the first day of integration.

As I bounced along on the front seat, I thought of the day this past summer when a lone black boy from Smithville had braved the city pool. He put his money down for a ticket and strolled through the locker room. "Big as life," Aunt Phyllis remarked. In his baggy red trunks, the boy lowered himself to the concrete pool's edge and tested the water with his toes. The moment his toes went in, the other kids hauled themselves out of the water. I watched from my towel on the grass, feeling, as we all must have, that we were doing wrong.

Frankie had seen it, too. He never went swimming but dropped by some afternoons to buy a Coke from the concession stand. He was there that day, sitting on a green bench in the shade of the bathhouse. He drank from his can, watching all those shivering kids on the pool's edge, the Smithville boy wading around the shallow end. Frankie crushed the empty can with one hand, tossed it in the trash as he sauntered out, not even looking my way.

Our bus hissed to a stop in front of the school. They'd carved up the old Woodford farm, blacktopped a curved drive to the top of the hill, and built a brick, two-story high school with long hallways running to every department. We entered through the glass doors, stood in the gleaming terrazzo lobby, and

Afterheat

were amazed. The first few weeks of school, everyone was nervous about fights breaking out, but beyond whispers in the bathrooms, school commenced in peace. All of a sudden, there were girls in my classes named Norvetta, Tijuana, and Raven.

"Eye-to-eye contact," our science teacher Mr. Browning admonished us on the first day of class. "Show me what you're made of!" Mr. Browning would start out talking about the steps of scientific inquiry but veer off into a lecture about how to be good citizens. He told us to scrub ourselves until our skin tingled like they did in the army, and to pick up litter even if it belonged to a stranger.

"You *can* learn algebra," Miss Stella informed us, her eyes wide and menacing. "And if you can work an equation as long as this blackboard, then you'll know you can do anything." She always pointed with her middle finger, apparently unaware of what it meant. Chinchilla Gay sat behind me, the girl from the brown-shingled house.

Mr. Browning and Miss Stella convinced me. I finished my algebra homework victoriously. For my science report, I researched atom bombs and radiation. I read everything in the Vance City Library and from the smooth-paged encyclopedias at home.

"According to Einstein," I wrote, "when an atom splits, the mass of the fragments produced is slightly less than the mass of the original atom." I pressed my pencil hard into the notebook page, straining to understand. "The difference in mass appears directly as energy. Energy is equal to mass times light squared. For the optimum displaced mass, a heavy atom, such as uranium, is used. At high velocities, only a small amount of mass is equivalent to a vast amount of energy. At the velocity of light, mass becomes infinite, length becomes zero, and time stops." I was terrified by the idea of time stopping. It had felt like that in my body cast, lying completely still so the grafts could take.

Most of the new students joined band. Our music department featured a soundproof complex of rooms for chorus and instrument practice and a large band room with six octagonal-shaped levels descending to the conductor's platform. The flutes and piccolos were closest to the conductor, then the reeds, then French horns, trombones, and trumpet players, James among them. Tuba players and drummers lined up in back.

Most of the band lacked expertise on the arpeggios and grace notes that only the brilliant

Afterheat

clarinet section could handle. Mr. Sponcil beat the podium with his fraying plastic wand. His spittle lashed the flute section. "Count out the sixteenth notes," he said, exasperated. "ONE-ee-and-uh. TWO-ee-and-uh." I sat next to Jade Tipton, twice my size, coffee-and-cream complexion, wide-thighed and dangle-earringed. Based on tryouts, our band instructor, Mr. Sponcil, assigned me first saxophone, first chair; Jade, first saxophone, second chair.

Every morning, Jade plunked herself down next to me, rattling the metal stand as she arranged her sheet music, then spread herself luxuriously over her folding chair to get her bearings. After our first concert, Mr. Sponcil announced that we could challenge the person one up from us for that chair. Right away, Jade put in her challenge. Our face-off was scheduled the day before Thanksgiving. Every day when we returned our instruments to their velvet-lined cases, Jade stared at me, sizing me up, psyching me out.

Every afternoon I settled myself onto a concrete block in the backyard and blew the notes of "Birth of the Blues." I played and practiced till I could play all the way through with my eyes closed, my teeth grinding out blood from my lower lip, my brother lobbing water balloons at me and shouting that I was driving him insane.

The challenge took place after school. Jade went first, a jazz medley, but her reed squeaked twice. When it was my turn, I adjusted my mouthpiece and opened the music on the stand. "Better to be strong and wrong," my Dad had advised me. My fingers moved clumsily at first, my first notes wandering, then I hit my stride.

Mr. Sponcil rubbed his weak, stubbly chin while he decided. "Close," he said. "But Ruby gets to keep her chair. Jade, you can challenge her again in three months if you'd like."

I packed my saxophone into its case and almost tripped out of the band room. I gathered myself and walked slowly down the hall, to the snack machine at the far side of the gym. My right hand trembled as I fed change into the slot and pushed the buttons for a package of Nip Chee.

Rounding the corner, I spotted Jade, still wearing her instrument. It hung from its neck strap and banged against her stomach. She unhooked her saxophone and held it in one hand above her head, drew her arm back, and hurled it all the way across the lobby. Flashing in an arc, it turned once in the air, then

Afterheat

crashed, bell first, and spun across the floor. It rolled all the way to my feet—bent bell, the shiny black mouthpiece with its thin, broken reed pointing at me.

The Nip Chee went dry in my mouth. I picked up her saxophone, gold with white pearl keys. It smelled of spit and metal, just like mine. I crossed the lobby and handed it to Jade, who cradled it like a baby.

"Congratulations. I'll get you next time," she said, her cinnamon eyes smoldering.

Each bus ran two loads of kids in the morning. We early kids waited in the gym until the late buses rumbled up the hill one by one. Some senior girls talked the principal into letting them set up a record player so we could dance until the bell rang for homeroom. One rainy morning, the bus stopped in front of the brown-shingled house and Chinchilla got on, wearing one of her starched pastel dresses. I was shocked when she quietly took a seat next to me, placed her feet in front of the heater bolted to the floor behind Mrs. Barrows. I stared at the beads of water on her patent-leather shoes quivering under the heater's fan.

I stole glances at Chinchilla's small hands and translucent fingernails, as she opened her notebook. I was afraid to look at her up close.

"You ready for that vocabulary test?" I ventured.

"Not really," Chinchilla said, her voice high and sweet. "I'm trying to learn these big old words right now."

"You always get everything right," I said. "Seems like you were born knowing algebra."

"I don't get straight A's," Chinchilla said. "My momma's liable to wear me out."

After that, I saved the spot next to me for Chinchilla. Mrs. Barrows studied us suspiciously in the rearview mirror. Chinchilla and I traded homework and snickered when one of the fancy girls tripped on the stairs or the boys' fists flew and Mrs. Barrows had to stop the bus and give them a talking to. One morning I forgot my pencil and Chinchilla gave me a stub of one from her old school—navy blue with DuPres imprinted in silver. Still, when we scrambled off the bus, Chinchilla beelined to the other black girls who congregated at the far end of the bleachers. James and his friend Doug climbed to the top row and slouched around, shooting rubber bands at girls from their fingertips.

Then one morning, during a long wait for the second-load buses, Chinchilla appeared beside me.

"I love this song," she said, "Wanna dance?"

Afterheat

I followed her cautiously to the bottom of the bleachers, where I kicked off my shoes behind the painted red line and ventured onto the glossy gym floor. We passed the glamorous seniors, jitterbugging in their lettered cardigans, and joined her group doing the "Mess Around" in a circle around the free throw line in their sock feet to "Please Mr. Postman," by the Marvelettes.

After that, I woke early to get my school clothes together, running the hissing V of the iron into my skirt pleats, pressing the powdery spray starch into the creases of my collars. Bus-duty teachers began watching us doing all the latest steps. They twitched their shoulders and snapped their fingers in time to the music. Chinchilla and her friends teased each other about their boyfriends, but I didn't mention Frankie.

The day of the Snowflake Invitational Basketball Tournament coincided with the Christmas parade. Our marching band strutted down Main Street in our red-and-gold uniforms with fringed epaulets. The DuPres kids had taught the rest of us their moves, so Jade had taken over my spot as rank leader, playing with that bent bell the whole time. We stopped in front of the courthouse and advanced into formation in the square.

We struck up our fight song, leaning, bowing and high stepping, twisting the bells of our trumpets, tubas, and trombones without missing a note. We moved as one body, a jolt of heat in the frigid day. When we finished, we stood at parade rest in our uniforms. A marching band is like the military—face-forward, perfect synchronization, expressions neutral. As the crowd applauded, I surveyed them in my peripheral vision. Little kids up high, straddling their father's shoulders, a knot of tough downtown kids, smoking, smiling in spite of themselves. Everyone had to admit it: since integration, the Clay County High School band had gotten good.

At the game that night in our new gym, our cheerleaders stood facing the home crowd, waving their arms in exaggerated X's, hushing us from booing the referees. We kept freezing the ball to stop the other team from scoring, but we lost anyway, 62 to 58. After the game, we band members returned our instruments to the music department. Heading back, I spotted Frankie's car from the entryway. In spite of myself, I waved my friends away and swung into the passenger's bucket seat, my band suit buttoned snug around my chest. Frankie bought me a chipped ham sandwich and French fries at Parkette Drive-In where

Afterheat

a gigantic neon sign in the shape of a carhop leaned out over the new freeway. We drove out Stepstone Pike and parked in the tree-enclosed rest area near the underpass. The skin of Frankie's lips was soft and sweet like the skin of marshmallows, but his touch was heavy.

"You feel it now, don't you?" he whispered, lifting my hair from my neck.

"I think so," I whispered back, but I was lying.

With Frankie, I learned to do a lot of things without feeling them. But I did them anyway. My silence about boys made Mom afraid. When she questioned me, I refused to answer. More than once, she lost patience, slapped me, or accused me of something. Still, I did not answer.

That night, I recounted the game to Frankie, how the tall forward sank a two-pointer at the buzzer, and about the halftime show our band performed. The story was true, the sweaty gym, the swaying crowd, but it felt like I was watching it all from a distance, like someone looking down from the top row of bleachers, someone from another town.

Frankie listened intently, drawing long puffs from his cigarette, his body zipped inside his mechanic's suit. I elaborated, my voice hoarse from yelling, blisters blooming on my fingers from clapping against my heavy class ring. I knew Frankie wanted me. His desire crept inside my veins like melting solder. I never wanted this grunting heaviness, sticky flayed flesh. Boys were the packages winking under the tree, never opened. The thrill was the shining ID bracelet and plush pile of the sports letter on a sweater. The thrill was the promise. I clutched Frankie from behind as he gunned his motorcycles down curving country roads. I never wanted him, but to fly like him.

When Frankie dropped me off at the sock hop, his fingers pressed into my forearm. "Wanna ride out in the country with me on Sunday?" His face registered exhaustion and need.

"Got to study." I always made excuses. I had track practice. I had band rehearsal.

He parted my teeth with his spearminty tongue and I thought how, years before, I'd wanted him to say this means you're my girlfriend. But he always left me there, alone in the clubhouse, the barn, the back of the truck, racing off to get swanked up for his real dates.

"Let go," I said, and wiggled out of his embrace. Frankie smoothed my face with his calloused fingers and blew a column of air across my neck. "So shiny."

"No, really, Frankie," I said. Anger closed my throat. He dropped his hands, but grabbed my wrist.

Afterheat

"Look at you, Miss Marching Band, Miss Nigger Lover," he said, flicking the crimson fringe of my epaulet. "I'm just a grease monkey. Is that what you think?"

"For Godsakes," I said.

Inside the darkened gym, I scanned for Chinchilla and Rosa. Music pulsed through the dancing crowd. I felt a hand, warm and soft, leading me. Jade. When we got to her group, someone helped me pull off my heavy band jacket. Someone else placed a small box in my hands. As my eyes adjusted, I saw tinfoil wrapping, and inside was a pair of big silver hoop earrings like they wore.

"Come on, girl," Norvetta said, helping me hook the earrings into my ear. The whole pack of us got up and danced. We jitterbugged, hands clasped together, we boogalooed. They taught me their dance steps and I showed them how to wildly agitate their hips like the Tahitians.

"You crazy," Jade said.

Sweating, we sat on the bleachers and watched the slow dancers.

"I remember when you got burned that time," Norvetta said. "I saw it in the paper."

"Me too," Jade said. "You were just a little

thing."

"What you talking about?" Raven said. "She still a little thing."

The scale of the explosion was so vast that witnesses reported very different perceptions, depending on their vantage points. From the rear of the bomber, the tail gunner peered down into what resembled a cauldron of boiling molasses.

Chapter 9
The Search for Wendy Starr

By my freshman year of high school, the Carousel Lounge's reputation had grown and was now considered a worthy little sister to the big steak places in Lexington and the fish houses built out over the river. Those restaurants sometimes flooded in spring, water rushing up the pilings, submerging the dining rooms. When the rains came, the Carousel doubled their stock orders and opened their doors to the overflow of customers looking for a serious catfish dinner.

In his imported Italian shirts, pressed slacks, and sandals made of woven leather, Forrest Bellamy cut a striking figure as he took his dinner at the Carousel. Forrest had finished college, done his duty in the Asian jungles, and returned home sound, sleek, and strong, eager to start his life as a gentleman farmer. He

Afterheat

was single and he was a Bellamy, the only son who'd decided to stay in Vance and work the old family farm: train horses, raise tobacco, harvest hay.

"I'll have the rib-eye dinner, medium rare," he said when I watched him order from Wendy one night. He gave her a little wink as he handed her back the menu.

She headed to the kitchen humming to a song on the jukebox, "Are you ready?" Barbara Mason's backup men implored in harmony. "Yes, I'm ready," Wendy sang along, loud as she pleased. Wendy Starr was considered fast. She'd developed what people called a cute figure, which meant full breasts, narrow waist, and rear end as luscious as a Georgia peach. She was not one of those plump cheerleaders with bare thighs and candied lips who implied promises they seldom delivered. Wendy always saw through to the sex of things.

So there it was. Forrest Bellamy, landed gentry, good-looking, well-off, the perfect catch for one of the country club cotillion girls, except that he liked Wendy, except that he asked her out on a date and six months later asked her to marry him. I imagined them riding in his truck down Ironworks Pike, the sun burnishing the walnut trees as they passed. Maybe he pulled over

CD Collins

and parked at the Pilot Knob lookout to watch the sun go down, took her olive-skinned hands in his.

"Wendy made her daddy nervous," Mom said to Aunt Phyllis, "because she made Forrest wait a month before she answered him." They chuckled over their iced tea as they sunned in the backyard. Forrest was twenty-three, ready to settle down, but Wendy hadn't even graduated high school. She wanted to think it over.

No one in town could believe it. They'd thought the little Starr girl was surely headed for the trailer. She'd marry some alcoholic ne'er-do-well and raise a rash of children on welfare. So they thought. There was all kinds of talk—it was a shotgun wedding; it wouldn't last. Yet it didn't matter what anyone said because Wendy attended her high school graduation wearing a diamond solitaire and now she ate her dinner on Saturday nights at the Campbell House in Lexington. She swam in the swimming pool at the country club in her bikini and moved into the big Victorian house out on the Bellamy farm. So what everyone said fell as dead as four o'clock.

The beginning of my college career was a model of poor planning. For me, college was an

Afterheat

abstraction. So on registration day, Mom just drove me to the University of Kentucky with a copy of my high school transcripts and I signed up. At the registrar's desk, an efficient-looking woman in a blue seersucker suit asked me what my major was. Nursing? Education? Home economics? She surveyed me in my cutoffs and long, pool-bleached hair. I wondered if she knew that seersucker meant milk and sugar.

"Science," I replied.

We drove home, packed my clothes, and I moved into an off-campus apartment with five other girls because the dormitories had all been filled. As a science major, I learned the names of things, how they worked, and my world drew into focus. In the hospital, no one looked me in the eye or told me the score. I'd lain in bed crying, watching dancers on *The Ed Sullivan Show*, convinced I would never walk again.

We'd overheard that our chances were fifty-fifty. I wanted to know what that meant, exactly. If I was not going to make it, precisely what would kill me? I found out that if half your body burns, there are a hundred ways to die. Third-degree burns are full-thickness burns, which melts all the way down into the fat, rendering flesh into crisp pieces, like crackling on pork roasts.

Overwhelmed, the body covers open wounds however it can. Scar tissue, like emergency glue, caused contractions so powerful that they can overcome any muscle power, and confine limbs to a permanently fixed position.

In class, I found out there was the issue of salt, that it had been necessary to shrink my cells through osmosis with a hypertonic solution, a mixture of half orange juice, half salt. The nurse had woken me every hour, steadied the straw while I drank, more salt than my blood could hold, it seemed, more salt than the ocean. Too much salt, my capillaries could burst and I could hemorrhage internally; too little, my body could weep to death through its wounds.

I took notes as I ate hash browns and eggs at the Tolly-Ho restaurant, while "Hey Jude" played over and over on the jukebox. I surveyed pictures of irradiated children from the heavy books I carried around in my knapsack.

I found out that in the decade I was burned, the 1960s, the likelihood of survival was 50 percent for pediatric patients if burns covered 35 to 44 percent of the total body surface area, and that few patients with burn sizes greater than 45 percent survived. I read that the leathery scabs that formed from burned

Afterheat
or cauterized skin was called eschar.

I learned that in Hiroshima, people close to the hypocenter of the bomb suffered third-degree burns, but at ground zero, the thermal radiation exposure was fifteen times what is required for third-degree burns, sufficient to cause exposed flesh to flash into steam.

In our off-campus house, we called ourselves women, not girls. We held sensitivity training sessions in our living room and the bearded boyfriends who ate dinner at our table helped wash the dishes. I wore bell-bottomed pants around campus instead of the Villager skirts and matching cable knit sweaters I'd worn in high school. In class, I spoke up, expressing opinions I didn't even know I had.

Sophomore year, my roommate, Belinda, showed me how to smoke marijuana, and we made a plan to drop acid. Different batches appeared in town—chocolate chip, orange wedge, windowpane. Tall and solid with long, sweeping dark hair, I admired Belinda's confidence. She got us some purple haze and informed me that everyone needed a guide on their first trip. She'd be mine. We rose at five o'clock, chewed the little square of paper with a raised purple dot at the center, and walked across the quiet campus to the Tolly-Ho. Belinda ordered orange juice and I ordered coffee. I'd drunk enough orange juice for a lifetime.

"Take this," Belinda said handing me a rose hip tablet.

Vitamin C was supposed to level off the big initial rush.

"Are you going up?" Belinda said to me after half an hour, her eyes dilated.

"Your irises are spinning like pinwheels," I said, falling forward into their vortex.

"You're starting to peak," she said. "Let's go."

Outside, the birds in the maples in front of the library began speaking in a language that I understood. Bliss and iris, bliss and roses, they chanted, a fugue of robins and wrens. The office tower compressed itself and then sprung skyward like an accordion. Overwhelmed, I knelt on the ground and covered my eyes with my hands, but I saw dark-haired girls floating on purple bubbles behind my eyelids.

One October evening, Belinda and I drove to Boonesboro Beach to camp before the frost. Old and slow, the Kentucky River is banked with steep limestone palisades and the largest system of caves and aquifers in the country. When we arrived with our backpacks and

Afterheat

gear, a party was already under way. Long-haired men and women wearing psychedelic colors were building a bonfire in a shallow pit. Candlelight flickered from the sandstone boulders. Janis Joplin's voice wavered from a tape deck rigged onto the hood of a yellow Mustang where dancers gyrated in a circle and people were crawling in and out of the caves. Under a tree, a lone couple swayed, slowdancing in their bare feet.

Belinda walked straight into the crowd and soon I heard her laughter skipping above the murmured conversations. I was pondering how Belinda thrived on crowds when I heard a low, melodic voice call my name.

I turned to face Wendy Starr lounging on a blanket at the mouth of a cave. She motioned for me and I clambered down.

"Little Ruby Chambers," Wendy said, patting a blanket for me to sit next to her. "What are you doing at this wild party?" The timbre of her voice was as rough and rhythmic as a bass line.

Wendy was so close I could feel her warmth, take in her grassy scent of vetiver. Like me, she had on bell-bottomed jeans, but instead of a T-shirt she wore a knit blouse with deep V and pattern of sparkles shaped like a comet.

"Going to UK," I said.

"In college," Wendy said. "That's what I heard. They teaching you anything you want to know?"

I told her all about macrobiotics, my course in feminism, driving to Washington for a war protest. "We got caught in a blizzard in the mountains," I said. "Sliding around the cliffs in a little Datsun with seven people and no heat." I buttoned my jean jacket against the cool breeze kicking up off the river. "What about you?" I said. "I hear you practically own Vance now. Got you a farmer. Got a farm."

"Looked like I hit jackpot, didn't it?" Wendy pulled a joint out of her purse. "But, baby, it was a prison." She lit the joint, took a drag, and handed it to me.

I pinched the rolled paper between my forefinger and thumb. The orange coal crept unevenly toward my face, popping a seed as I inhaled the harsh smoke. I blew out quickly, hoping I wouldn't get high. Pot could flip me over into panic. Smoking marijuana made me think of the Beatles lyric "Hold you in his armchair, you can feel his disease; come together . . ." We would all die young anyway, we protesters of the Vietnam War, we forgers of the Revolution.

Wendy took a deep draw from the joint, held

Afterheat

it, and then exhaled it with a sigh. She told me that yes, she'd fallen in love with Forrest, that he was a kind man, a good man, who'd tried hard as he could. She wanted to make it work, too, but had given up her young life only to be absorbed into his. "I didn't have to push anymore," she said, "Maybe I need the friction." She'd begun to resent him, she said, to hate him, even. "Sometimes I didn't go home, stayed out all night at the Catalina motel. I'd show up the next afternoon and of course he'd want to know where the hell I'd been."

"Does he know where the hell you are now?" I asked.

"Guess you haven't been to Vance lately," Wendy said. "We signed the papers last month. I told him all I wanted was a red Cadillac, enough cash in the glove compartment to get me to New York City, and a divorce.

"You're leaving?" I said, startled upright. "By yourself?"

"Sweet little Ruby," Wendy said. "That silky hair, those sea green eyes, searching so hard. Try to enjoy yourself a little. Tomorrow morning I'm going to put the top down on my convertible and floor it out of here. I might disappear, like a Rockefeller. If I go, I'll go the same way he did, on an adventure. I left Forrest, and even if I'll be sorry tomorrow, I'm glad today."

A man with pumped-up arms and fatigue pants emerged from the shadows. "Hey there," he said to Wendy as he folded his arms over his chest. "I know you."

"Hey," Wendy said, smiling up at him. "You look familiar."

"We met at that big plantation party over in Vance," he said. "Devon, remember? Listen, I've got a good set-up back in that cave over there. Nice down bed, smokes, moonshine. Sleeping bag big enough for two, three if your little buddy wants to join us."

"Thanks for the offer," Wendy said, "but I'm catching up with my friend, Ruby."

"Now don't give me that," the man said. "I know what you're here for. Come with me, and let me jog your memory."

"Like I said, Devon," Wendy replied. "I'm enjoying myself right here."

The man leaned forward and whispered menacingly, "Well, you can go straight to hell," he said.

"I'll see you there," Wendy said, following him with her eyes as he staggered back toward the caves. "You know," Wendy said to me, "I got up every day and dressed in that old dark apartment above the

Afterheat

restaurant. I tiptoed down those stairs so I wouldn't wake my parents, passed beer taps and ashtrays, liquor bottles lined up along the mirror, got my lunch money out of the cash register. I walked to school up the trash-strewn sidewalks of Locust Street, drunks curled up in the alcoves waiting for the bars to open. Even they looked sideways at me, felt sorry for me. Not a single tree on my street, not one true friend. I tried not to let anything they said stick. But Lord, I felt the weight of it. I think Mom felt the weight, too, when she went rolling down those stairs."

Wendy glanced at me, and I fought an impulse to look away. We all speculated, including me.

"People think Daddy pushed her," Wendy said.

I stayed still, hoping she'd continue. But she stared into the bonfire. Someone threw on a piece of driftwood and sparks sprayed up into the night.

"I know you were in the hospital when Mom passed, on the verge of dying yourself. But I'll tell you this. Those stairs are slick. They are covered with grease from the exhaust of a thousand catfish dinners. They are old and they are worn. It's harder to keep your footing than it is to slip."

"The night before I left for my honeymoon, I made Daddy tell me what happened. He said Mom had confronted him about some deals he'd been making, sending runners on the pill highway back and forth from Florida, vote buying. He denied everything. He admitted that his lie was like playing poker where he dealt himself five cards and her four, but kept saying it was five. He was her husband. She trusted him and it made her crazy. He told me that she left that night wearing a flowered dress, her face crumpled. He didn't follow her, but instead finished off his bottle of Old Overholt, real quick like. The next thing he knew Deputy Garrett was shaking him and calling his name. Daddy says he doesn't know if it happened as she was leaving or if she was trying to come back."

"What do you think?" I asked her.

"I saw how he treated her. Pushed her in a thousand ways. But here's how I see it. I've fallen down those stairs, too. You just have to make a little misstep to send you tumbling. Everything drops into slow motion, and you think you can hold out your hands to the walls and stop yourself from falling. You really believe it. But you can't stop. You just keep falling and falling."

In my physics class, the professor had drawn a diagram on the board, with a stick figure, an incline, and arrows. He'd explained that momentum isn't just

Afterheat

speed and velocity, but velocity times mass. A small force applied for a long time can produce the same momentum change as a large force applied briefly. French and Italian have no single word that combines the concept. Motion times power times mass. They refer to the phenomenon as quantity of motion.

"It's the momentum, isn't it," I said. "You can't fight the override."

The party grew and the music crested, Jimi Hendrix's wailing guitar echoing through the caves as fireflies floated among the pine branches.

"Government has nerve gas stored in there," Wendy said. "Your momma knows all about it. You go into one of those caves and get lost, find out it's full of poison. You might think someplace is the safest place in the world and it turns out to be the most dangerous. You can sneak around the edges of your own life and hope that no one notices you, but that's being dead already."

The Kentucky River flowed silently by the karst towers and columns, fissures, and caves surrounding us. Belinda had disappeared, probably into one of the caves.

"Dance with me," Wendy said.

I followed her, the soft sand and pine needles under our feet. She stared right into me with her slanted, made-up eyes. Her thick, blunt-cut hair swished over itself when she moved. I saw why Forrest could not resist. There was an excitement about her, a willingness to jump, reaching into the night, keen for experience, even if it was pain. At the end of the song, she held me close, pressed her body against mine, and held me around the waist.

She held for an extra moment and looked me square in the face. When I met her gaze, my body jolted with current she sent out that could electrocute a person on the spot. I had always wanted to go with her, to follow her sparkling comet as it hurtled through space. I could have reached for her, held her waist in my two hands, as thin and dense as a paperback book.

When the fireball expanded, a wave of compressed air pushed out, producing a vacuum. Since sound requires a medium of travel, those in the epicenter saw a flash, pika, but heard nothing, while those in the outskirts of town observed the flash, then heard the roar, pika-don, flash-boom.

Some saw pink light; others saw white, golden, blue, scarlet, or green, depending on their relationship to the waves of light, whether the waves were moving toward or away from them, and through what medium they were being refracted, according to quantum theory. Astronomers can also detect the motion of stars through a spectroscopic telescope, the fleeing reds and approaching blues.

Chapter 10
Home Fires

Nowadays, fire follows my father around—his houses burn, cars, barns—he keeps moving. Everything burns. Even trailers, even the house he built himself from chunks of limestone. I lived in that house. One day we came home and there was nothing much left but rock walls. His suits in the closet had curled up and shrunk on their hangers. That year he had worn pastel suits, and now they hung in the closet like smoky mints.

After that, he moved alone to a farm in Bath County. When that house burned, we found out he had listed my mother's missing rings on the insurance as part of the destroyed property. Someone said that one of my dad's girlfriends was wearing those rings.

Today he glides down my driveway in one of

Afterheat

his Cadillacs. Bethel, his eighteen-year-old girlfriend, sits delicately beside him. She always wears a dress. She has about a bushel of frizzy dark hair and heavy-lidded eyes. When she smiles, I notice her dark teeth. She never speaks outright, though she sometimes nods or whispers a word or two. He has never introduced us. When the Bath County School burned down, my friends and I naturally thought of Dad. Somebody joked that maybe Bethel had gotten a bad grade.

I walk out to meet him but he doesn't look at me. I know something's wrong because he rolls down the window without looking at me. I sneak glances inside to where Bethel sits on the honey-colored leather interior. Today, her patent-leather shoes are white and she has a matching pocketbook. Dad slides the gear into park and turns off the key. He glances at me through the car's open window. He has come to fight.

"Clell told me you wouldn't let him park in your driveway," he says, his mouth tightening. He doesn't have lips anymore, just a soured place. Clell is my father's right-hand man.

Each year, my father hires Clell and everyone in his extended family to cut, house, and strip the tobacco that my father raises on my farm. Part of the

CD Collins

allotment is mine, but I never receive compensation for it. Every year is the same. My father begins the summer with comments about how good the crops look, how he turned in the best hand of tobacco at the fair. Then after the November sales he says, looking past me, "Came up short. Blue mold was bad this year." Or "house burn," a rot condition when the weather's too wet. I let him raise the crops anyway. I used to believe the blue mold stories, then I figured it out, but what I couldn't figure out was how to buck the routine. Saying no to my dad tends to have consequences.

In early spring, Clell's family migrates the twenty miles from Lucky Stop to my farm. They come at six in the morning with country music screeching out of their radios. They stay all day, roaring around the fields on tractors. Around eleven o'clock, a couple of them go to McDonald's or Wendy's and bring back lunch for everyone. After they eat, they pitch the bags into the field. Around dusk, they rumble out again in their jacked-up trucks, station wagons full of kids, and old Impalas without mufflers. When I go back to check the new tobacco beds, I come upon nests of aqua Styrofoam boxes and pinkish milkshake cups.

Every time Clell gets thrown in jail, my father puts up his bail. The driveway dispute is a symptom of

Afterheat

the long-standing privacy problem between my father and me.

My father is looking out the front windshield at the crushed blue gravel in my drive. The gravel is new, Number 9. "I don't understand you, Ruby," he says. "I try to help you, but you're always on my back."

"He can use the other entrance," I say. When my dad finally looks at me, he has a shocked expression like I'm someone he didn't expect to see. He primly points out that it has been raining. Did I want the whole damn field torn up?

"Claytis," Bethel says in a low voice and looks sideways at him.

"Answer me!" my father swears as he grips the steering wheel, then pushes off from it to climb out of the car toward me. Bethel leans after him. "You bitch," he says to me.

Now, at fifty-five, my father is an almost tiny man whose overall color seems to be getting lighter and lighter to match his lit-up eyes. He still has small smooth hands, but his hair is turning from brown to a withering blond; he has thinning legs and a little bit of a belly, like a sack of sugar.

I try to let his words roll off me.

"I need my privacy," I say.

"Well, I can sure as hell see why you need it," he says. "If I had friends like yours, I'd want to hide them, too."

I thought about the fact that Clell Stiles just got out of prison for armed robbery and suspected arson. My mom told me when he came to the farm to definitely avoid him, "He's mean, Ruby," she said, giving me one of her long-term looks.

The first time I saw Clell, I was taking a shortcut through the Belks' parking lot. An auto shop let out into an alley and I saw my dad's white Cadillac inside the parking lot. I walked up to it, thinking Dad might be in there. When the mechanic turned around, I saw a handsome face and the name Clell stitched into the pocket. Remembering my mother's words, I thought Sweet Jesus, how do I get out of here, but he smiled and asked me if I was looking for Claytis. He didn't seem especially mean to me, but he had a watchful silence that stilled the air around him.

The next time I saw him was at the election party my Dad threw in my house. When I came home from work, there were cars parked all over the yard. Clell was in the kitchen drinking my sherry from the bottle. When he saw me, he dropped the bottle to his side. It dangled from his hand while he swayed, red-

Afterheat

eyed, with half a smile drifting up the left side of his face. "Well, I'll buy you some more, honey," he said.

In the living room, Dad was sitting on the couch with his arm around Bethel. There were a bunch of men who looked like variations of Clell and a few women dressed in bright colors. Everyone was watching TV, eating peanuts, and drinking beer. It was the night the Zapruder film of the Kennedy assassination was first shown on national television. They played the home movie over and over—the motorcade, the pillbox hat, the pink mist of his brain.

I went back outside and climbed into the old Chevy farm truck, and gunned it into the field by the pond. I felt like a criminal driving in the field. I parked facing the house. Ray Stacey dropped by later, and we sat in the truck with our feet propped up on the open doors. We watched the house and smoked. Ray was my friend, so I thought he had to take my side. But I wasn't sure of him.

What finally motivated me to put in the second entrance was my orange kitten, Rafter. One morning I couldn't find her. I walked around the yard till I saw her lying in the long grass, completely flat. That afternoon, I went to the barn and told the men that they had run over my kitten. I had to yell up to the top bent of the barn because they were all up there steadying the rails so they could hang tobacco. The radio played "Heaven's Just a Sin Away." One of the Stiles boys shouted down, "Sorry. We didn't see her." I stood there till they came down. "It was a bought cat," I said. "Long haired."

Billy Stiles asked me what I expected she was worth. I said about twenty dollars. The men stood around looking down, smiling a little to each other. Billy said he'd bring me the money the next day. He didn't, of course.

That summer, I had the entrance built. If it rained, it meant the men had to park their cars and walk to the barn or use my driveway, which was closer.

My dad knocks down another beer and tosses the can in the grass. He leans up against the Cadillac and points at me with his right forefinger. "Your so-called friends are using you, Ruby," he says. "Can't you see that?"

"Leave my friends out of this," I say. "Everyone needs privacy. Apparently, you do. I don't even know where you live. I've got nothing against your friends, except when they roam in and out of my house."

"They never go in without me," he says. I think, Oh great, like that's supposed to be a comfort. I think about the nickel-plated gun that used to be in my

Afterheat

underwear drawer. My father and his Velcro fingers.

"Do you think I don't know what goes on out here. That Ray with his big, ugly beard," he says, biting his words. "How do you think him being in and out of here all the time looks on you. And what does the son-of-a-bitch do for money?"

"I think that's Ray's business," I say.

My father rolls his eyes. This eye rolling is a family trait. Even my brother's little boy does it at two. Then he laughs through his nose, meaning, "I rest my case."

During the next half hour my father claims that he will slit the throats of all my friends, set my house on fire, and see to it that I lose my job. "I got you that job," he says, going for another warm beer. He seems to be strangling on his words, like a dissatisfied horse trying to spit out a bit. I've heard most of this before. It's just a variation of his usual: the Claytis Chambers Approach to Family Enlightenment. I stand, trying to let the words blow around me like a bad wind. I notice how my father's teeth have gotten ground down, yellowed like hard field corn. I don't mention the prison records of his friends.

I tremble, but I tell myself that today the story will end a little differently. I guess I am just at the point where getting pushed around feels worse than taking a chance. On what, I don't know. I walk toward the house, move inside, lock the door, and call the Clay County Sheriff.

My father rattles the plastic window, barely secured to the door with caulking. I am talking to the police. Is he there now? Is he threatening me directly? I have to make a peace bond and then catch him at my farm. I need witnesses. I repeat that he's here now. He has guns in his trunk. He might use them. They are sorry but he has to shoot first. They are sorry, but they don't like to get involved in domestic problems.

My father is still scratching at the door. I part the curtains. "I won't hurt you," he says.

He didn't always look like this. In his army picture, his hair is full and wavy, blue-white eyes, brows, heavy but pleasing, like sleeping foxes, and an almost humble half smile, tipping his head to one side.

I part the curtains again. I don't look away. He calms. I open the door.

"I think you should leave," I tell him.

"I ain't going nowhere."

I walk past him on the cistern stoop. Bethel sits waiting in the open car. I've never spoken to her, but I lean down and ask her if my dad has been drinking a lot

Afterheat

lately. She looks sideways at me and whispers, "Yeah, quite a bit."

I ask her what she thinks we ought to do. "Call Berry Mae," she says. My dad's sister.

Berry Mae is there in five minutes. She talks to my dad in the yard while I sit in the car with Bethel. We don't talk so we can hear them: "Now Junior, this keeps up, somebody's going to get killed. You go on back home."

Then she comes over and looks in on Bethel and me. "Honey, why don't you get away from that old man," she says to Bethel.

"I ain't got nowheres to go," she whispers. She says she doesn't want to go home because her daddy won't leave her alone. "Claytis's good to me. You know he can't do nothing." Her mouth drops open into a gray smile.

My father appears. I climb out and let him have the driver's seat. After Berry Mae is out of earshot he starts the car. "I meant what I said. Nobody crosses me, including you." Then he backs down the drive. Another family trait, backing long distances in cars.

"I think you're making a mistake," my mother says when I call her on the phone to tell her I am going to sign a peace bond to keep my father off my property.

"He's going to die soon anyway. Why take away the only thing he has left?"

"I've got no choice about this. You stopped putting up with him ten years ago." I feel light and empty. I don't know if I can do this without my mother's blessing.

"I know. I know," she says. "But he's still your father."

"Was Bethel with him?" she asks. I tell her yes. "Could someone do what he's doing for . . . lust?" Like lust was something people outgrew.

I tell her I think Bethel is probably better off with my dad than her own. "Look, Mom," I say, "I need your help. I mean, if this thing goes to court, would you stand for me."

In the silence, I can feel her receding through the wires. "I can't help you, Ruby."

The next day, I call the District Attorney. They don't recommend this. Am I sure I am willing to face my father in a court of law? Wives and kids tend to back out. I ask if I have the legal right to keep him off my property. Well, yes, I do.

Okay, first, I have to catch him there. He has started to come only during the day when I am at work. I ask Ray if he can drive by my house on his way

Afterheat

to the afternoon shift at Bluegrass Industries.

"Yeah, sure, but what if I see him?"

"Call me at work," I say. "I know it's a lot to ask."

A few days later, I look up from my desk at the high school. It's Ray. He has that gray-white skin he gets when he's scared. I call the police.

When I get home that afternoon, the grass in my front yard is all pressed down, and I wonder if there has been a scuffle. I wonder where my Dad is. I imagine his shock when the policemen rolled down the drive. I call the jail. Jimmy Fawns, the deputy, gets on the phone. He tells me that he served the warrant and incarcerated him for a few hours before letting him go if he swore to show up in court.

"He didn't have his medicine on him, Ruby," Jimmy says. "You know he's not real healthy."

I ask him what I'm supposed to do now and he tells me that they have to set a court date and let Judge Duvall decide.

On September 14, I ask my friend Janet to cover my sixth-period General Science class on her planning hour, and leave school at two o'clock. Inside the courtroom, my mother sits in a pew in her tailored dress and Greta Garbo hairdo. She tends to be glamorous and dramatic whatever she does.

I sit on the bench beside her without speaking. It is quiet and dusty in the cherry-paneled courtroom. She gives me a resigned smile. My father comes in and sits on the other side of the aisle one bench back. I think, let's just all go home and forget about this.

I notice Micah Fritz is the court clerk. Guess she got promoted from taking pictures for licenses. Bet she can't wait to go home and spread this dirt. Still, she seems impartial. She hears this kind of thing every day.

The hearing itself is pretty painless. The county attorney talks for me. My dad's lawyer talks for him. He's not allowed to drive any of his Cadillacs in my private drive as of now. Judge Duvall wants to know if I want him to continue raising crops on my farm. The judge has mottled red skin and spiky black and white brows. I went to school with his son, Robert, who was diagnosed with schizophrenia. He is waiting. Yes. He can raise his crops there. I know it's his sole income. But he'll have to start buying his own insurance for the barns. I know if I stop paying for it, he'll pick it up. My father is a big believer in insurance.

We leave the courtroom one at a time. My mother doesn't have to testify. She waits for me and

Afterheat

holds my hand going down the courthouse steps. I used to hate her doing that because both of us have dry skin and it hurt. But not today.

Sometimes, my father still drives one of his Cadillacs down my driveway. He never comes in, just drives through the gate and closes it behind him. He usually uses the other entrance. He drives up from the barn to the fence to hang sacks of vegetables over the post in plastic Kroger bags so I'll notice and come to get them.

This morning, after I put the coffee on, I stood in the back door watching the pink sunrise in the fog. I see my dad driving up in a Cadillac. Today, he has two bags. As I watch him, I remember how in love with him my mother was. The way he danced with her, we could tell he thought she was just about the prettiest woman alive.

I've ridden in his Cadillacs a few times. One hard winter when I was out of work and the snow was two feet deep for weeks on end, he came to get me and drove me to the grocery. I had a bad case of cabin fever since it hadn't gotten above zero for nearly a month and by the time he came, I didn't even want to go out. He drove evenly down the soft, white roads. From inside the car, I could hear nothing except the faint squeak of the tires pressing down the snow. A pine-scented deodorant board in the shape of a Christmas tree swung from the radio knob. "Kroger okay?" he asked. I said that was fine and he sniffed, a nervous habit of his that meant everything is under control or this is the end of the conversation. He stopped the car in front of the store, slid one hand out of its rabbit-fur-lined glove, and handed me twenty-five dollars.

Now I watch him limp toward the fence. I can see that his boot is only partly zipped. Gout. The rich man's disease. His hair is getting long. The way he combs it makes one side much longer than the other.

He hangs the vegetables over the post: onions, beets, peas, squash. Later I know there will be cucumbers, beans, new potatoes; then in July, corn, tomatoes, sweet potatoes, melon.

One summer James went away to band camp, and Dad and I went fishing at Chalk Lake, just the two of us. I trailed my feet in the boat's wake out into the middle of the lake. We rocked there all afternoon with the dry oars up inside the boat. He pushed the worms on the hook for me, piercing the chain of hearts. We caught sunfish, bass, and bream, piling them in the minnow bucket. We ate bologna and crackers and

Afterheat

something my dad called rat cheese, a yellow cheddar with holes in it. We kept Cokes and Miller High Life in a bag off the side of the boat to keep them cool.

On the way home from the lake, we drove over the tip of the Appalachian Mountains through Stanton and Campton toward Natural Bridge. My father told me that one day we would have a picnic in the sky. We would sit on the clouds and the sky would be our table.

That night my father grilled the fish and my mother poured me glass after glass of milk. She stood smiling while I drank and drank. I felt like a boy. This is my happiest memory.

Now I see him leaving the bags on the fence, turning to go. I know our limits. Once, he said I could have anything I wanted. I believed him. My father with his oaths, his curses, his promises.

Chapter 11
The Gold One
Pearl

Pearl Lovelace Chambers stood in her carport with a digging trowel in one hand as her ex-husband, Claytis Chambers, pulled up in his 1977 Cadillac. She wondered if anyone besides a dreamer like Claytis had ever taken the notion to rehabilitate his own car without knowing the first thing about auto body work. Today, there were long strips of masking tape covering the chrome and squaring off the hood ornament. On the roof, something that looked to Pearl like cake frosting gleamed in the sun.

Claytis fished in the trunk for a bulky paper bag. When he closed the lid, it groaned like an old man taking a stomach punch. "This town's just like Los Angeles," he said. "Everybody has to drive."

Afterheat

Pearl moved closer to examine the Cadillac, the stiff waves of her hair damp and askew. "Vance, Kentucky, is a long way from Los Angeles," she said. "Thank the good Lord."

In 1977, the manufacturers of luxury cars were still expanding their models, and though this one had escaped grasshopper fenders, its length was enormous (126-inch wheel base, as Claytis pointed out), the seats a rolling expanse of leather in whose folds you could lose your wallet. Claytis had owned this car forever, and now the foam roof had rotted, the back seat had been worn to tatters, and the gold paint on the body had chipped away. Last month, he'd driven around town with a rusty primer coat over the Bondoed fenders.

Claytis tucked the bag under his arm. "Well, what do you think?"

Pearl ran her fingers across the white roof. "Hmm…" The roof was rough-textured like a stucco of Marshmallow Fluff and cement. She tapped it with her trowel.

"Invented this stuff myself," he said. "Next goes a black coat."

"Umhmm…" Pearl turned on her heel and started up the sidewalk. She had better things to do

CD Collins

than stand listening to Claytis' nonsense about that car. She admired his spunk, though. She didn't know anybody else who lived on $250 a month Social Security and managed to drive a Cadillac Eldorado.

Claytis followed her up to the porch, explaining that he'd already put five coats of gold on his car and wouldn't be through till there were nineteen. Seems that all those coats gave it depth, like staring into golden outer space.

"Well," Pearl remarked, holding the screen door for him. "Tea?" She laid the muddy trowel on the kitchen table next to her cut-crystal ashtray and went to wash her hands in the kitchen sink.

"Please," he half yelled above the sound of running water. "If you've got some made."

As Pearl put on the kettle, she thought about the fact that Claytis had bought a new Cadillac every year until 1977 when the floor began to drop out of the housing industry, and they'd both happened to be standing on it. He'd just built five beautiful homes on the best ridge of the farm they'd hocked their socks for, and there was no one even to make a bid. Not to mention he'd run into what he called a low point in his luck cycle at the horse track, bought too many steak dinners and cocktails for supposed friends, and even

Afterheat

he admitted that he'd let his drinking get out of hand.

Claytis rummaged in the paper bag, pulling out a two-pound sack of sunflower seeds, about twenty seed packets, and something wooden that resembled a wall sconce. The pictures on the seed packets promised long, perfect cucumbers, glowing summer squash, clusters of exotic purple beans, and snow peas nestled among curling tendrils. Pearl wondered if any of this stuff was intended as her birthday present.

Not that she expected anything from him. Not that her birthday was anything special, although she'd bought herself a little something this morning. In fact, birthdays in general made her cross. All she'd gotten from James and Ruby was flowers, as if she needed flowers in summer. Pearl felt sorry that her own children had the imagination of cinderblocks.

But she had received one little present in the mail that morning, Bain Creme Lavande, it said on the bottle, from Will. He wrote inside the card that he hoped that someday they could visit a beach like this one. She studied the picture on the front of the card: fine white sand and enormous curling waves. She knew what people would think seeing them together, a beautiful young man and an older woman. Will was from Connecticut, and when they'd first started up he'd teased her about her middle name, Lovelace. He said he didn't like the way people down here pronounced it Loveless because he wanted her to be loved more. After that, he always called her Lacey. She studied the contents of the bottle, translucent and heavy, pale purple swirling in on itself. He was always giving her something pretty.

Pearl didn't know what Will saw in her. Maybe once, an older woman for curiosity's sake, but their wildness had been going on for over a year. The last time he was here, she'd looked into his eyes, fern green with flecks of amber, so full of life and information. He never disappointed her the way other people did, herself included. She wondered what he saw when he gazed into her too-knowing eyes, her lined, sorrowful face. After their nights together, she was always afraid Claytis could tell what she'd been doing or that he would catch them together and make a scene. Then Will would never come back.

Nobody really knew about her and Will, even James, who had introduced them. James was showing her around the vocational school where he was building a model barn in the carpentry department. They happened upon Will, who was wiring the barn in preparation for getting his electrician's license.

Afterheat

She could tell immediately that Will wasn't from around there. He had a self-contained way about him, as if he couldn't care less what people thought of his shaggy curls, his leather knapsack, and his tight jeans. He walked like he was sort of proud of himself. Will had driven her and James up to Red River Gorge and wore her out hiking. They'd gone all the way up to Lukigee Rock, a wide platform of sandstone where on a full moon you could watch the sunset to the right, then a few moments later, the moon rising on the left. Pearl sat cross-legged on the sandstone, between the two of them, as the sky darkened to indigo.

"I hope to God somebody brought a flashlight," Pearl said, realizing she would never make it down that steep little trail in the dark.

"Don't worry," Will said, laying a warm hand on her knee.

The first time Will stopped by her house, he brought some kind of crusty homemade bread and chocolate bars. "This is what I always ate for lunch in Europe," he said, tearing off two handfuls of bread and laying the chocolate in between. "Bon appétit."

Pearl was impressed. She had always wanted to go to Florence. She found herself telling Will about things Claytis would have laughed at, like how she lay in bed at night and imagined her soul flying up to the stars. When Will kissed her, she kissed him right back even though she knew he'd be moving soon, and did again every time his contracting job in New Haven sent him down this way. Mornings, they drank the special sweet-tasting coffee he kept stashed in his knapsack, then shooed him out a good hour before the time Claytis usually came. She closed the door so she wouldn't have to watch him drive off.

When Pearl heard Claytis' car in the drive today, she stuffed the gift, card, and wrappers into her vanity drawer. On second thought, she pulled a flannel dust rag over all of it and shut the drawer tight. If Claytis ever found out, he'd die—right after he killed the two of them.

Pearl set Claytis' tea, thick with cream and spun honey, on a straw placemat. She examined the sconce.

"It's a squirrel feeder," he said. "If we poke an ear of field corn on the post, a squirrel will come sit on the little bench and eat his lunch."

"And smoke his pipe afterward, I guess." She blew a stray curl out of her face. The light coming through the door illumined Claytis' eyes: star sapphires. She'd fallen in love because of those eyes.

Afterheat

As he aged, his hair had paled and his face had become smooth and pink. She still didn't know whether he was pulling her leg or not on any given subject. He spliced facts and lies so well together during their marriage that she never figured it out till the bills came or the bank foreclosed. And if he kept talking, sometimes not even then.

"Well, I guess we'll leave it up to the squirrels, won't we?" he pursed his lips and took a swig of tea. He ate and drank as if food and drink were dirty substances he didn't really want to touch. He was like that about a lot of things. For example, the subject of his young live-in girlfriend, Bethel, whom Pearl found out about through local rumor.

But when James reported to her that his dad was sleeping on a bed that looked like it might collapse in the middle, she couldn't bear the thought of him suffocating in the night. She ordered new box springs and a mattress and frame. When she met the movers at Claytis' apartment, a quiet, slender girl let them in without so much as a hello. The girl wore a halter top and cotton shorts and tucked her dark head in like a terrapin. Pearl could see that the girl had been mistreated in more ways than one.

The apartment was about what you'd expect

for fifty dollars a month above a diner in not the best part of town. Dark, cramped, reeking of yeast and grease. Its cleanliness was about the only thing that recommended it. Pearl was shocked by the order, everything in its place, the tabletops and counters polished to a sheen. In the kitchen, long wooden shelves held dozens of jars of canned vegetables from last year's garden. The girl followed her at a distance. After a few minutes, Pearl realized that the long pauses between her questions and the girl's answers were not due to her taciturn disposition but to the length of time it took her to form responses in her mind. She was slow. Pearl wondered if she cooked. She wondered if Claytis still had his male trouble.

Pearl lugged the sunflower seeds into the backyard and swatted a gangly black kitten off the cement table. "Waiting on a cardinal, aren't you, Preacher?" She unhooked the feeder from a limb of the dogwood tree and worked off the plastic top. "Nothing will please you but a fat, lady cardinal," she said to the cat, then to Claytis. "I save two or three every day. Yesterday, he got a bluebird. Had its head right in his mouth."

"Pound's a good place for a cat like that." Claytis sliced open the seed bag with his pocket knife.

Afterheat

"Any cat for that matter." The seeds clattered into the feeder with a sound like falling coins.

"Don't you listen, Preacher," Pearl said, but the cat had rounded the corner of the house, its tail riding high. When she rehooked the bird feeder, blue jays cackled and swarmed around it.

Pearl rested on the cement patio bench and smoked the first of five cigarettes she allowed herself per day. She drank cold black coffee in a china cup while Claytis finished his tea and foraged for sticks to use as row markers in the garden. There was very little left to mow in Pearl's backyard since she'd planted so many flowers. She confessed to having gone wild with bulbs this year. In March, she'd planted twenty-five black parrot tulips in one of the few patches left. Then, dead center, she planted big red Oriental Poppy.

Claytis nailed the supposed squirrel feeder as high as he could reach on the trunk of the biggest apple tree and attached the dried corn. Then they started on the garden. In early April, they'd planted greens and lettuce underneath a tobacco cloth, and put in a row of beans. Pearl's mother told her that beans planted on the hundredth day of the year always thrived. Her grandmother used herbs and flowers for various ailments and was practically considered a healer. Now,

Pearl wished she'd listened to her grandmother's recipes better. She wanted to know how to take fire out of burns and ease bursitis, but as a girl, she'd been preoccupied with boyfriends and nail polish.

She did remember about the beans, though, and the ones she and Claytis planted on the hundredth day were already flowering. He liked to plant a new row every two weeks so they'd have beans all summer and into the fall. Last week, they harrowed up the side garden with Pearl's rototiller, working over the soil six or seven times, raking last year's weeds out of the way.

"Claytis Chambers! You watch out for my hollyhock roots," Pearl had yelled over the sound of the motor.

"Flowers in a vegetable garden," he complained, cutting the engine and examining the soil. "Taking up space."

It was true that each year there was less room for the vegetables, but that suited Pearl just fine. She was much more interested in looking at something pretty than she was in eating, anyway.

Today, Pearl held her stick tied with string while Claytis paced gently to the end of the row, and dug in his stick, the string straight and taut between them. Together, they marked off half a dozen rows. Claytis

Afterheat

then angled the hoe blade and dragged perfect furrows down the rows. Pearl followed along, dropping hard white beans at intervals into the fresh, black soil. When she'd finished, he covered the bean seeds, tamping the loose dirt with the flat face of the hoe.

Claytis had an elegance about him, an eye for the essential thing. The way he worked this garden as though it required no effort—divide the soil, plant, cover, press, no wasted strokes. He didn't waste any energy on regret, either. Even when they had lost the subdivision, and finally the Bath County farm.

She remembered that night so well. High summer. She and Claytis were getting ready to drive down to the river for dinner. He'd come in with that red-bronze look he got when he'd been fishing all day in the sun. He showered and dressed in his white shirt and black slacks, still so good-looking, though his eyes were already bloodshot from beer. She'd worn her gardenia-print dress with bright fuchsia lipstick and matching heels. He told her that she looked like a Tahitian princess. They looked so handsome that even James and Ruby seemed proud of them, teasing them and snapping pictures with the Brownie Starmatic. "Bank's got everything back," Claytis had said, buffing his wing tips. "It's that simple." She'd gone to him and cried, kissed him; they were in this together.

After the divorce, she'd gone back to her old government job. Through sheer determination, she managed to hold on to her house and a few antiques. She had her backyard and her orchard sloping down to the quarry. She had the trees, big and mighty now, the ones they'd planted when the house was built. It was awful the way contractors these days scraped off the topsoil, built cheap houses on hard clay where nothing could take root. At least Claytis had never done that.

It wasn't till she'd divorced him over carousing that it dawned on her that girlfriends and liquor were the least of his lies. From bits and pieces of gossip and what Claytis dropped while not thinking, she realized he'd been selling off lots for low-dollar cash and gambling away the money. He always denied everything until it was a dead subject. She'd wanted something different from her marriage, something good for James and Ruby and something true for herself. She watched as her husband's life became ragged, putting up bail for his no-account friends who pretended Claytis was as big as he thought he was. She'd had her heart broken so many times it felt all scarred down, as if it couldn't be hurt any more. She was always surprised when it could, and she didn't like surprises.

Afterheat

Pearl watched him moving easily back and forth with the hoe. The sun was high by the time they'd finished the row planting, Pearl was sweating and her back hurt from bending over. "Want some lunch?" she asked him. But he wanted to go ahead with the squash and cucumber hills and the long built-up mounds for the carrots and beets.

For an instant, Pearl imagined grabbing the hoe and smacking the smug back of his head with it, but she grumbled to herself instead and lit a cigarette, leaving it stuck in the corner of her mouth. "Fine," she said, and kept on working. The smoke collected in her hair and burned her eyes. The beet seeds were in tiny, easy-to-lose clusters and the carrot seeds were a nearly invisible tweed pattern in the dark soil. Trying to concentrate on spacing them gave her a sick headache.

When they finished, Claytis clapped dust from his manicured hands. He wasn't even sweating. "I'll be by later," he said.

"Why do you always say that?" Pearl said, irritated. She leaned the hoe against the shed. When she turned to him, the hoe slid into the grass. "You say that every day and you never come back." She stamped toward the house, narrowly missing a patch of lilies of the valley. "Not unless you want something."

CD Collins

Pearl didn't know if he heard that last remark or not because she went into the house and closed the door. He'd gotten the muffler fixed, so she didn't even hear him leave. She didn't like not hearing him coming or going. When she locked the doors on her way out somewhere, it was Claytis she was locking them against. At least his car was running, and she didn't have to shuttle him back and forth. Last week, she had to pick him up downtown every day after his errands. One day she couldn't find him in the rain; then she'd spotted him on the steps of the Church of Christ, holding a dripping newspaper over his head. She leaned across the seat and unlocked the door. "Better not get too close to the church," she'd teased. "They might drag you in and teach you a lesson." He hadn't said anything, just climbed into the car with a rueful smile. He'd looked so small, then, in his thin shirt and rain-spattered khakis.

Pearl pulled a fried chicken leg out of the refrigerator and poured herself a glass of lemonade. She smiled when she thought about him stranded on the church steps like a wet rooster. She should have killed him when he was twenty-five and kept him perfect in her heart forever. Pearl drank the lemonade and poured another glassful. Ruby said she used too

Afterheat

much sugar, but that's the way she liked it. If you couldn't have your pleasures in life, then what was the point?

Her eyes wandered over the glassware on the whatnot shelves flanking her sink—the hobnail pitcher, the grotesque little Toby jug, the Italian wine goblet with the satin-glass stem shaped like Bacchus. She lifted the glass, holding the miniature body in her hand, perfectly shaped, naked except for a cluster of grapes between his legs, the laughing head crowned with a garland of leaves. With Will, she entered a world she could imagine, of this goblet, of a universe without rules, sublime and free. She placed the goblet all the way to the back of the shelf, safe from being accidentally shattered.

She stared out the kitchen window at the blue jays, craving a cigarette. She'd wait, didn't want to go all evening with just two. In the cherry tree, a jay held a sunflower seed, wedged it between its feet, pecked out the kernel, let the hull drop to the ground, and retrieved another. She couldn't imagine how the bird got that kernel without toppling headfirst off the limb. She wanted to do that sometimes. Just let go, fall.

She carried her lemonade down the hall to sip during her bath. That was one thing she didn't skimp on, personal care products. She poured an overflowing capful of the new bath creme into the running water and fastened up her hair with bobby pins. Here she was, sixty years old and alone, just like her mother predicted. She'd learned one valuable lesson from her mother, the one about not getting your hopes up, but she'd learned it late. Maybe she could learn a lesson from Claytis, too. Smile at yourself in the mirror sometimes, forgive yourself.

After her bath, she wrapped her robe around her and lay down on the day bed in her sunroom. The pale blue robe was an elaborate damask of buds and vines, the last gift Claytis had given her. She had been shocked on Christmas to find something she truly liked; hard to find, too. That year he'd bought fancy watches for James and Ruby. "Next year, I'll buy you both cars," he'd promised, believing it to be true. Claytis' dreams had never died. He knew someday his efforts would pay off, and when they did, it would all be for her and James and Ruby. This was never the love she wanted, but it was Claytis' form of love.

She nestled into the pillows and drew deeply from her third cigarette. When Bethel and the deliverymen left her alone in Claytis' bedroom, Pearl had noticed a card on the dresser. She couldn't help

Afterheat

herself. On the front, Santa and his reindeer rode a trail of crystal sand into the sky above a sleeping town. Inside, in a childish scrawl was written: "Dear Claytis, you are the true man. I no I am a luckie woman."

Since then, Pearl had heard bits of gossip about Bethel——Bethel thought she was pregnant, but it was really a tumor; she'd run off with the sacking boy from Foodtown; she'd been hauled off to Eastern State Mental Asylum; but Pearl hadn't actually seen Bethel since that day in the apartment.

Pulling her robe around her, she wondered what Claytis and Bethel talked about at night. Did they laugh, hold each other as they slept? Smoke curled among the philodendron leaves, drifting into the sunshine in slow swirls. She stubbed out her cigarette in the amethyst ashtray. What right did he have, Claytis Chambers, to judge her one way or the other? He went home to someone every night while she was alone. She pictured Will living with her, hopping around like a sprite with his curls, his eyes sparkling, talking nonstop and baking that braided bread. No. Not Claytis; not Will, either. She was alone and would be alone, and with the cool release that accompanies acceptance, she fell asleep knowing that she liked it that way.

She was awakened by the sound of something

banging in the kitchen. She smelled burning charcoal. Claytis. With that new muffler, he could sneak up the drive when she was asleep.

"Told you I'd see you later," Claytis called from the kitchen. "Happy birthday."

Pearl got up, coughing. In the kitchen, he was basting something brown on two thick steaks laid out on the counter, next to several ears of corn wrapped in tin foil. There was the tender, dry smell of potatoes baking. In the drive, the enormous Cadillac loomed like a ship in the sunset.

"Remember what you fixed for dinner that first night after our honeymoon?" he rinsed the blade of a chopping knife and thin-sliced ripe tomatoes, arranging them in a semi-circle on a platter.

"Brownies for dinner." Pearl said. "That's all I knew how to cook."

"Good, though." Claytis checked the potatoes with a fork. "Black walnuts on top."

Pearl set the patio table and lit a citronella candle. By the time Claytis piled the grilled steaks and vegetables on their plates, it was nearly dark. Halfway through dinner, Pearl saw something moving out of the corner of her eye. In the chalky blue light, she could just make out a squirrel perched on the wooden sconce gnawing on corn.

"Well, I'll be." Claytis let out a self-satisfied chuckle and set a box wrapped in pink tissue on the table.

Pearl picked up the box and shook it, something small, but heavy. He liked to buy her shiny things: rings, money clips set with agates, charms. She removed the tissue and lifted the lid. A silver lighter gleamed in the candlelight, engraved with her name.

"But you hate it that I smoke," Pearl said.

"True." Claytis set up two lawn chairs side by side and blew out the candle. "Can't stop you, though."

They watched a half moon ringed with indigo rise above the trees in the orchard. The lighter sparked once and then burned bright. Cigarettes tasted best in the evening. Preacher jumped in her lap and purred till she put him down and fed him a steak scrap from her plate. He tried to jump back up, but she scolded him away. She didn't want him getting grease on her good robe. She loved the way the polished threads of damask wove underneath each other and then surfaced again to reveal a reverse pattern of light and dark on each side. It occurred to her that she and Claytis were that opposite, that connected. For the amount of time they spent together, they may as well be married. But she didn't say that. If she did, he might scamper off into the dusk like an animal protecting its wound. Sometimes she felt her own face shutting down, sadness tugging at the corners of her mouth.

She scooted her chair closer to Claytis,' but the metal frames bumped and left a space between them. "Thanks for dinner," she began. "But you know, sometimes I'm busy at night." Her cigarette was like a red firefly in the dusk. "Your place is at home. With Bethel." Pearl felt giddy, being so direct with him, like she was suddenly flying and hadn't known she could. She took another swoop. "You're not rough with her, are you?" Who knew what she'd say next.

Claytis rubbed his face as though ridding himself of an invisible web. "Did I ever lay a hand on you? The girl says things. You know she's not right up here." He tapped his head with his forefinger.

Pearl braced herself in her chair and went on to say that he ought to enroll Bethel in some night courses at the high school. "She might even earn a high school diploma someday."

He muttered that Bethel was happy where she was and that what he'd learned from books hadn't helped him one bit.

"Say you'll help her." Pearl said. "Unless you

Afterheat
want me to do it for you."

For once, he was silent, but she knew he was listening. She peered into the darkness for a moment, at the squirrel and the garden that lay beyond. She thought of the seeds underground that would burst open and curl up through the soil after the next rain. "Next week we'll put in the peppers and tomatoes," she said. "We might even get wild and put in an eggplant."

Claytis was very still. She could see only the outline of his face and the tilt of his head. She flicked her silver lighter and relit the citronella candle. In the sudden brightness, he looked young, his face scrubbed clean and fresh. She knew he would leave soon, packing up his things and walk slowly to his enormous, impractical car. She looked forward to her last cigarette of the day. She would smoke it lying in bed with the lamp off and window open, listening to the wind chimes she'd bought last week at Grayson's yard sale. She would allow the images into her mind that eased her into sleep. She would savor them, and then she would let them go.

"They had two lighters, earlier." His voice crackled as though after a long silence. "I wanted the gold one. But it was gone."

Chapter 12
Laundromat Jesus

"It's going to hit seventy today," Dad forecasts, opening the Vance *Sentinel* on my mother's dining room table.

My parents fought every day of their marriage, but since their divorce, they appear to be getting along fine. Both had a boyfriend or girlfriend or two along the way, but here they were back together, Mom in her mid-sixties, Dad in his late.

Mom lives alone in the rock house Dad built while my brother and I were still in junior high school; Dad lives downtown.

Outside, the weeping cherry tree blossoms like pink popcorn exploding down the branches. Last week, Dad nailed a giant plastic thermometer to its delicate trunk with a ten-penny nail. Sap runs from the

Afterheat

nail wound into a jelled clot in the lush grass.

Dad is cutting coupons out of the ad section. He is a bargain hunter when it comes to food. He's been known to drive the forty miles to Lexington and pack his car trunk with Scot Lad brand canned green beans, because, bought by the case, they came to only 11 cents per can. He's been known to buy out spice warehouses and country stores. "I don't even use curry powder, let alone a whole damn case of it," Mom complained, surveying her jam-packed cabinets. "Where in the hell am I supposed to put the salt?"

After the ads, Dad reads a column called Down Memory Lane, which highlights local events that took place on a particular date five, ten, and twenty-five years ago. He calls out people and events.

"Five years ago Pammy Kaye Kendrick was selected as Vance's representative to the state Junior Miss Pageant," he reads.

"Rigged," I say.

"Superintendent's daughter!" Mom calls from the kitchen where she thumbs thick pats of butter onto slices of Salt Risen bread.

"Ten years ago today, H. R. Reeves was named head of the Farmer's Bank," Dad reads. "Egotistical son-of-a-bitch. Twenty-five years ago, DuPres High

School burned down."

When DuPres, our all-black school in the east end of town, was scheduled to be integrated with Clay County, our all-white school, the tension grew so thick that everyone in the county predicted riot. Old Man Sturgill flourished an ancient revolver on the courthouse lawn, hollering about mulatto babies until he was escorted away by two state troopers.

The night before the fall term, someone set fire to the DuPres School and burned it down to its cinder blocks. The next morning, the first day of my freshman year, our bus made several extra stops and the former DuPres students boarded the bus in supernatural silence. I felt a kinship with the new students that I didn't fully understand until Mom happened to tell me about Ludie Quisenberry. Ms. Ludie took care of me from the time my mother returned to work, when I was two weeks old, till I was three years old. All that time, Miss Ludie had gotten by with wheeling my perambulator down the hill into the east end of town where I spent the day being rolled around the floor by her four children and fed home cooking. Mom had to fire Miss Ludie when a neighbor blew her cover, but my impressions had already been formed. Love, safety, and comfort lay in the arms of a black woman, and the

Afterheat

small black hands that stroked me in sleep.

"The whole downtown glowed orange," I say, about the DuPres fire.

"Stroke of genius, lighting that match," Mom says.

With no school for the DuPres students to attend, integration went off without a hitch. No arson arrests were ever made and the identity of the perpetrator remains one of several local mysteries. Dad turns the page and traces down the list on the Matter of Record section with his forefinger, looking for familiar names.

"Jesus got a DUI," Dad says.

Mom slides the tray of buttered bread under the broiler. "After all he's been through," she replies, "he probably needed a drink."

Mom keeps up with Jesus Martinez, who works in tobacco. He is one of a few hundred Mexicans who began moving into Vance about five years ago. She interprets his behavior as though it is an auguring method. If Jesus' name stays out of the Matter of Record for two weeks straight, she takes this as a sign of good things to come. When it reappears, she makes excuses.

"Last week he got arrested for terroristic

threatening," my father says, brushing a stray flower petal from the paper. "They should have kept him in jail."

Mom pours her third cup of coffee of the morning. "They probably just misunderstood what he said."

Dad straightens up and stretches his back. "Maybe you should go on out to Grassy Lick Hacienda," he says. "Draw him up some well water to drink."

"I can't believe you're jealous of Jesus," she says. She sips her coffee as she watches a humming bird siphoning colored sugar water from its feeder in the cherry tree. Leaning over the table, she scans the Matter of Record. "Dorothy Franks theft-by-deception," she reads to Dad. "Burl Romine, driving without an operator's license; Carl Cantrell expired insurance. These names read like your address book, Junior."

"I don't know what you're talking about," Dad says. He'd taught me this trick by example before I'd learned to walk: deny everything.

Dad's personality is a confounding cocktail of generosity, paranoia, the desire to be a big shot, and a need to hide. He is a giver, who seems to want us all to celebrate a party he's conceived and financed.

Afterheat
He envisions himself appearing for a moment, bowing humbly, and then retreating into his den to watch the game.

Growing up, I remember him as a solitary man who became sociable only when drinking too much, buying us extravagant presents as though that could make us happy. When that didn't work with his family, he tried a rougher crowd, but when the money dried up, so did his pool of so-called buddies. By then, his drinking had muscled his better impulses out of the way and he'd resorted to fists and bullets as strategies for negotiation. I'll never forget the sight of him staggering to the door with his shotgun, insisting that my friends from Washington, D.C. were holding me hostage, as evidenced by the boycott lettuce bumper sticker on their Volvo, and that he was there to save me. "*Kapow*," went the Colt .45 he pointed skyward in one hand; *thuumpt*, *thummpt* went the 12-gauge in the other.

"Says here there's a flower show tomorrow down in Carlisle," Dad smooths out the creases to get a better look.

"We could go for Mother's Day," I say, hugging my mother from behind. "Maybe James could meet us there."

Mom shrugs. She hates holidays almost as much as she hates surprises. "We could go shopping for some curtains for your farm," she says.

"I don't need curtains," I tell her for the 103rd time. "I like light."

"I hear they've got some cute shops up in North Middletown."

"I'd rather eat ants from a stick," I say.

Wisps of black smoke trail up from the oven and drift into the dining room. I whisk the toast from beneath the broiler and slide all six slices onto a plate. They are charred with wells of melted butter.

"Perfect!" Mom says.

Dad shakes his head. "Carcinogenic."

I wanted my parents to divorce for as long as I could remember. The whole notion of marriage and living together seemed all wrong for them even from my perspective as a child. When they separated, I felt only gratitude.

Now, my father arrives each morning at ten o'clock, reads the paper, and feeds the birds. They accompany each other to doctors' appointments; to Amburgey's Farm Supply for birdseed and lawn tools; to the grocery store. Most days, he drives home before suppertime.

Afterheat

Dad's world is laid out in a precise order. Monday, shopping; Tuesday, cleaning; Wednesday, laundry. Thursday, he irons his shirts and pants with a military crease. You cannot find a speck of dirt on my father's floors or under his fingernails, nor a single picture on his walls.

Mom's life is desultory and spontaneous, a jumble of beauty and neglect, the cut-glass vases with freshly cut flowers next to Rookwood ashtrays overflowing with lipstick-stained cigarette butts. Shallow pools of cold coffee languish in Limoge cups.

Yet, my mother is the more constant of the two, the iron hoof in the tattered silk glove. Last year, when the dentist reamed out the roots of Dad's worn-down teeth, she served him meals from her old-fashioned one-speed blender. Three meals a day, seven days a week, five solid months, until his new dentures arrived.

Dad closes the newspaper and folds it neatly. "If these Vance people got jobs, they might stay out of trouble. I don't understand them."

"They're too good to work for Jesus' wages," Mom says, folding the newspaper and tossing it into the recycle bin.

The next morning, Mom and I attend Mass

in the Episcopal prayer garden. A breeze carries the melon scent of peonies from the flowerbeds to where we sit on metal folding chairs set up in rows on the brick courtyard. In one corner, St. Francis of Assisi extends his granite hands, blessing the stone rabbits. Dogwood blossoms seem to float in the morning air. My Sunday school teacher once told our class of nine-year-olds that Jesus' cross was made from timbers of a dogwood tree. After the crucifixion, God put a blight on dogwoods, making them dwarfed and crooked so no one else could be crucified on one again. She said that the five crinkly petals represented the bloody palms, pierced feet, the Roman's sword mark in one side. We believed; the proof was in the petals. Same with sand dollars, the five white doves of peace inside. When Mrs. Colley brought in a sand dollar from Florida, we nearly swooned. Jesus was everywhere you looked.

To begin the Mass, Father John descends the slate steps in his most regal drag, flourishing a jeweled wine goblet toward heaven. He genuflects to the dry, translucent host in his magnificent ultramarine robe. At the end of his homily, he asks the mothers to stand and presents them with potted purple violas. I stand, too, even though my children have all been feline. If Father John's a father, then I'm a mother.

Afterheat

The flower show in Carlisle has nothing to offer that Mom's garden doesn't, except for a bank of bonsai trees. James revered anything Asian because of his interest in the martial arts, but I saw only torture. Bonsai start out as real trees, but are pruned until they become a fraction of what they could have been, like miniature ponies or bound feet. Mom, Dad, and I stroll the paths laid with green indoor-outdoor carpet, admiring velvet-throated gloxinia and drinking in overwhelmingly sweet breath of stargazer lilies. My parents scan the room for James, but he never shows.

On the drive home, I marvel bitterly at how James can dominate a situation either by his presence or absence. In high school, they bought him a new silver trumpet while I played the junky saxophone my uncle had used in a jazz band. I joined the Y-Teens, Girl Scouts, and Candy Stripers, running errands for nurses at the hospital. I was in the Beta Club and elected vice president of my class. All of this got five seconds of attention from my parents. I could take care of myself, they reckoned. James needed a little extra love.

"Maybe he's had a car accident," I say.

Mom skewers me with a laser look.

"Maybe his wife needed him to wash her car,"

Dad says, from the back seat. He's never liked any of James' wives.

James has left a message on Mom's answering machine. At the last minute, his wife was called in to work. As an ER nurse, Caroline was always chasing some emergency. My brother's breathy baritone reminds me of the taste of horehound candy. "Happy Mother's Day," he adds, like an afterthought.

"Why couldn't he just come by himself?" Dad complains, pacing up and down the hall, peering outside in case he'd decided to come after all. "He shouldn't be married," he says with his signature dry sniff. Today the sniff means that he'd declared that James should not be married and he would not take it back. Maybe he was right. In our family, marriage spelled trouble.

"Well, I'm going to the Laundromat," Mom says.

"On Mother's Day?" Dad asks.

"Dryer's on the blink," she says.

Dad looks hurt. He takes it personally when something goes wrong with the house. He'd built this house for her and installed the very best of everything, but it also meant that everything was decades old.

"You want to spend the evening with a bunch

Afterheat

of strangers?" He extends upturned hands like St. Francis.

"It's always empty Sunday nights," Mom says, flatly.

Dad and I exchange a look, shaking our heads as if to say, headstrong and heartless, just the way she is.

Mom's dryer is on the blink, but her washer works fine. After my father leaves, she and I lug five baskets of wet laundry to her car. This method creates twice the work of carrying the clothes dirty and dry, but my mother would break an arm to save a nickel. The Laundromat is not empty, but populated by a group of Mexican men, smoking cigarettes and reading *People* magazine.

One of the men glances up and rushes to help my mother. He is compact and handsome with smooth skin, his shoulder-length hair has the sheen of polished mahogany. With the help of his friend, they carry in all the soggy clothes and load them into a rolling basket.

"Gracias," Mom says to him.

He tips his UK Wildcat hat.

Mason's Coin-Op is an old-style washateria with framed instructions written in cursive script, No Dyeing in Washers, No Rubber in Dryers, and images of pleased-as-punch housewives in shirtwaist dresses.

When James and I were kids, doing laundry was our idea of a good time. We'd perch on the long folding tables amid the stacks of fragrant, warm clothes, relishing our nabs and Cokes.

As Mom and I load the dryers, I whisper. "Where are all the women?"

We slide quarters in the dryer slots and twirl the knobs to high.

"Home in Mexico, maybe," she says. "I never see them here."

The Mexicans are not migrant workers, but live in trailer parks out on Grassy Lick Road, twelve, fifteen to a trailer. Mobile homes, the salesmen call them, smiling like funeral directors. Single wides, double wides, Colonial style.

I use the extra quarters for a Baby Ruth and a Dr. Pepper from the snack machines, then settle in with a year-old *Cosmopolitan*.

After a few minutes, I notice the men murmuring to each other over by the steam-stained storefront window. One of them unloads a jade onyx chess set from his knapsack, centers the board on a Formica coffee table, and begins unwrapping each piece from a scrap of brightly-colored woven fabric—

Afterheat

first the blue men—rooks, knights, bishops, pawns, the lame but crucial king, the queen, whose power equals the bishops and rooks combined. Then the whites. The men glance expectantly toward Mom.

When she crosses the room, they offer her the seat in front of the white pieces, and reassemble into a loose circle, sitting, standing, leaning forward, peering over each other's shoulders to gain a good vantage point.

The Laundromat superintendent screws up his mouth in disapproval of the tableau. Charged by the electricity, the proximity of these men, I position my chair close enough to follow the moves. Mom opens with a Queen's Gambit—she loves to free that queen to get the game going, and maximize her trail of destruction. Blue counters surprisingly with a Caro-Kann, and the game is on. The men murmur to each other in Spanish, smiling and nodding when either contender makes a good play.

I survey the men, all of whom appear to be under thirty—a chunky one in blue jeans and T-shirt that reads "Just Do It"; a very dark-skinned handsome one with a neat goatee; the mahogany-haired one, leaning back, half-smiling with his arms crossed, as though enjoying a cool breeze that caressed him alone. Mom's opponent moves his pieces with delicate precision around the board, his hands skillful like a potter's. On the surface, the men appear courtly and mild. But then again, so does my dad.

"Sheckmate," a tall, craggy one says firmly after about fifteen minutes, declaring my mother the winner.

The next contender, Just Do It, slips into place across from Mom, who reverses the board, presenting him with the whites. I return to my magazine, lulled by the whirring *ka-thunk* of the dryers. I imagine Dad's face distorted with rage glaring through the Laundromat window. Again the gun, again the wrongheaded drive to defend his family. This time I would not cower, not flee my house in the middle of the night to hide away on my friends' floors.

My vigor has exceeded theirs, already we were changing hands, shifting from their dubious protection of me, to my equally uncertain succor. If I saw Dad's hand raise a weapon in malignant righteousness, I would hold out my hands and he this time would relinquish his weapon to me.

"Do you come here every week?" I ask Mom when we are in the car, the laundry stacked and warm in the back seat.

Afterheat

"Not every week," she says.

As we pass the Coin-Op, I search for the men through the storefront, but see only our own reflection driving off in Mom's old Lincoln convertible. Two single women, small but willful, fair-haired, wiry. From a distance, practically the same.

Or maybe. If Dad had happened to walk by tonight on his way to Kroger's to buy tomato plants or marigolds, he would have seen Mom, and pause for a moment in awe. Marriage didn't last in my family, but love was indelible, like a name scrawled with a laundry marker on the deepest fabric of our being. Maybe he wouldn't have grown angry, but simply admired that discordant combination of audacity and shyness that had drawn him to her so many years ago: a woman who would play chess with a group of strange men no matter what anyone thought, yet never introduce herself, never ask their names.

Jesus, driving without an operator's license—
Jesus, failure to appear—
One of them was bound to be him.

Chapter 13
Free Enterprise

William and Tonya Alfrey (pronounced Aw-free) stand on the back porch watching their unnaturally beautiful children play in the ragged yard. The Alfreys rent my house for $200 a month. They are late on their rent. Again.

William is telling me about the Impala in my garage, his pride and joy. Would I mind if he brought in another car?

"1966 *Mustang* convertible," he says, reverently. "Classic baby blue. Real collector's item." William's smile is missing a few teeth.

Up close, I can see William's skin has coarsened from harsh weather and years of Pop Tarts, barbecued pork ribs, and Iron City beer. I remind him that I'm doing him a favor by letting him use the garage at all.

Afterheat

The original deal was to keep it padlocked so I could store the furniture that I couldn't jam into my studio apartment up in Boston.

"I don't know, William," I say, stalling. "First, clean up all these tires before they make donuts of dead grass all around the yard. And you've got to get the rent to me by the first of the month. Okay?" I've always had trouble with a simple no.

William nods, shifts his toothpick from one side of his mouth to the other with his tongue. "I plan on painting the house this summer, if that's okay with you." William explains that his brother can get the paint real cheap, plus new columns for the front of the house. "The old ones are kindly rotted."

I've heard this story before, from the people who rented the house before the Alfreys. They would replace the shutters and gutters, plant an orchard in the old corn field. All this in exchange for a lower rent. In the year that couple lived here, the house slid further into disrepair and the lawn grew a fine crop of polk weed. That couple disappeared before winter set in, leaving me thigh-deep in a yard full of snakes, their names, "Jim + Rosie," spray-painted along the plank fence. Before them, there were some methamphetamine producers who also raised rabbits in the house.

The Alfreys' platinum-haired daughter rounds the house, leading a dusty, miserable-looking Rottweiler with a piece of fodder twine. "Stay," she says jerking at the rope. "Good boy."

"Heather Marie, be gentle," Tonya chides her daughter. Tonya is having her own tug of war with her ruffled blouse—trying to situate it high enough to cover her ample breasts, low enough to drape her bountiful hips.

Most people who rent in Vance seek newly built apartments with central heat and air conditioning, not drafty, rambling farmhouses, or so I was told by a local realtor. I chose the Alfreys because both parents had jobs as opposed to living on public assistance like the other applicants.

Tonya works as a short-order cook at Jerry's Restaurant. "I wouldn't eat there for nothin'," is Tonya's review.

William works for the highway department, picking up trash and sawing limbs from between telephone wires. For safety reasons, the department won't let the laborers wear gloves, so William's hands look like they've been caught in a corn thresher. At twenty-nine, his body is bent, his face wizened. I've

Afterheat
known William his whole life.

This farmhouse, where I lived the years between graduating college and moving into my Boston studio, is equipped with four bedrooms, four fireplaces, tiger oak mantle pieces, poplar floors, and twelve-foot ceilings. It is a wooden-frame house sitting on a stone foundation with a wraparound porch, a Victorian cottage built in the 1890s. It is nestled among shade trees and surrounded by a fifty-six acre farm. Chopping wood for the stove, keeping the roof plugged, and on and on. Hard to live in, hard to keep up with. I'd ruined my body on it. I'd gone to auctions with my mother and furnished it with period antiques. After I left, the tenants carried them off, one piece at a time.

When I first moved to this house after college, I'd catch sight of William out my kitchen window, a wild child tearing through the fields and fishing bass from my pond with a cane pole. He spent whole weeks in summer with his grandmother, who raised peacocks on her property that ran along the railroad tracks behind my farm.

William actually lived downtown on Mitchell Street, in one of those dirt-yard houses rented to families who walked to work at the box factory. When those families failed on rent, they moved two streets over and rented a similar ramshackle house from a different landlord. To celebrate their new start, they'd buy their kids' plastic Go-Karts at Maloney's Discount House and make another dirt-yard out the back door, if there wasn't one there already. They put infants' playpens in the yard, too, and blow-up swimming pools two inches deep that collected gravel and urine all through the long Popsicle-soaked afternoons.

That was a long time ago, though, back before the box factory closed, around the time I'd thrown a lawn party on my farm in celebration of my golden birthday, twenty-two on the twenty-second of July, and William looked just like one of his movie star children.

I tease William and Tonya, telling them I envy their living in my house for $200 a month while I live in one room with nothing but concrete and delivery trucks outside. "Thousand dollars a month," I tell them.

They blink with incredulity. "Remind us not to move up there," William says.

Rural-dwelling Southerners have as much trouble imagining a reason to live in polluted, overcrowded crime havens like Boston and New York City, as urban-dwelling Northerners have trying to fathom why anyone would live in a culturally deprived hinterland with neither cappuccino nor ocean.

William Jr. races by vigorously bouncing an under-inflated basketball in the driveway. He hurls the ball high against the side of the garage, aiming toward an imaginary hoop.

"Doesn't he look like William just shat him out?" Tonya's smile reveals spectacular cavities. "That's like a metaphor, Ms. Chambers. Or like you might say, a carbon copy."

Tonya was one of my students her senior year of high school.

On the first day of the term, I doggedly taught all my classes the lowdown on the elements in chronological order: name, atomic number, name of discoverer and why the elements were important at different points in history. "Think about it," I'd encourage them. "Copper, gold, lead, silver, iron, carbon, tin."

Across the hall, my friend Janet taught them the names for literary devices—assonance, alliteration, onomatopoeia, the difference between a simile and a metaphor. It pleased me that at least Tonya remembered that there was such a thing as carbon, such a concept as metaphor. I wondered if she remembered dysthenesia, the concept of the disordering of the senses. The evening smelled chartreuse. Dysthenesia was a good term for how it felt to witness my property disintegrating before my eyes, the rotting eaves and sagging porch, the encroaching tangle of wild roses, and, most disturbing, the eerie quiet of the pond. Used to be, that between the bullfrogs and the crickets, I had to wear earplugs and run the box fan on high to get a good night's sleep. But one summer, the bullfrog chorus diminished by degrees. By late August, the pond had gathered serenely into a mossy, green stillness, punctuated only by an occasional truck with a faulty muffler and the forsaken call of the peacocks like a child in a well.

"I'd say William Jr. is the spitting image of his daddy," I say. "Both cute as bugs."

"You think so?" Tonya says, checking William out with a doubtful expression. "Well, you can have the daddy. I'll lend him out to you."

Husband borrowing has always been popular among the single women of Vance for tasks requiring manly heft. "Can I borrow your husband?" Roxie Harris used to sing to my mother, her aristocratic head angled

Afterheat

from behind the privet hedge. "I'll bring him back."

"I meant that literally," I say to Tonya. "Cute like a potato beetle or a June bug."

William smiles, as though proud to be a June bug, tenacious and iridescent. "Well, if you change your mind…" he drawls.

"Cute as a tarantula," Tonya interrupts, elbowing William in the side. "Thoughtful as a cockroach. I have the best dream where I chase him down and kill him."

Tonya and William stand arm-in-arm on the back porch watching their children poke at a hornets' nest with a tobacco stick. I look above the children's heads, past the grove of white pines toward town.

I don't live in Vance anymore. One day, I looked out the second floor window of my classroom, where I supposedly taught chemistry and physics to high school seniors, and felt my life narrow to the size of the scene below me—rough East End boys, the Taulbes, the Goldirons, the Franks, huddled under the smoking shelter sucking on Marlboros in the rain. All the years until my retirement would hold that view, and the one inside my classroom, each year's slew of students looking progressively younger, then graduating and, if they could afford it, blowing this pop stand—Vance,

Kentucky, population 8,547 tiny, little minds.

It was horribly unfair, I thought, watching one of the boys crush a Marlboro underfoot. My auspicious teaching career suddenly appeared like a life sentence—Sergeant Chambers, as my students called me, incarcerated here in Building One, drumming the periodic table into unwilling seventeen-year-old heads until the day I died.

Just before spring break, one of my seniors, who closely resembled Carrie Fisher as Princess Leia, said to me, "Ms. Chambers, I think it's time we both graduated from Clay County High."

A few months later, that was exactly what I'd done; I rented out my farmhouse and ran away from home to Massachusetts. That was four years ago, and not a day has gone by that I do not thank Princess Leia.

Tonya graduated a few years before I left, but William had dropped out his sophomore year, the same year his little cousin, Butch, died. When Butch learned that he'd failed first grade, he vomited at recess. Crying and embarrassed, he ended up strangling himself before the playground duty teachers noticed there was trouble over by the jungle gym.

Tonya withdraws into the house to shuck up some rent, the battered screen door slapping shut

Afterheat

behind her.

"You don't happen to know who gigged all my frogs, do you?" I ask William.

"Lately?" William's eyes cut across the shambling fence toward the pond.

"No, back when your Grandma Alfrey was still living," I say. I don't say back before your no-good father auctioned her farm off for a quarter of what it was worth and drank through the proceeds. "You Alfrey boys probably love frog's legs, don't you?"

"Now I caught some bass in that pond," William says. "But I always had your permission. That's a deep water hole, like a funnel." William draws the heels of his hands together to form a V. "Catfish too, big as my arm. But I never gigged no frogs."

William fishes in his pocket and produces a pack of gum. He slides a stick up with his thumb, offering it to me. It's Beeman's, my favorite brand, which I haven't seen in years.

"All of them disappeared," I say, accepting the gum. "I thought that was greedy." The wintergreen flavor diffuses through my taste buds, improving my mood.

I went night-gigging once with Dad, spotting the shiny backs with a flashlight, thrusting a spear into the adrenaline-frozen frog with a small, heavy pitchfork attached to a long pole. You had to be decisive and fast. Some people used spring-trap gigs, where all you had to do was touch the frog to clamp its bulgy body between pinchers. Spring traps were considered bad sport.

"I shorely don't know a thing about it. No ma'am," William says, shaking his head as though deeply saddened by the collapse of the bullfrog kingdom. William's eyes flash up at me, still full of sparks. "But if I ever find who done it, I swear I'll help you get even."

My seventeen-hour car trip back to Boston is financed by the five twenty-dollar bills Tonya thrust into my hand, apologies and promises whispered into my ear. In my studio apartment, I pull out my old yearbooks and look for William. In his eighth-grade picture, he sits up straight and bright, beaming for the camera. By his freshman year, he looks exhausted and his mouth crimped. Sophomore year, they don't even list his name.

I close the annual and gaze out at the single tree that provides nature for the thirty-some apartments that face it. Maybe I should have boarded my house up like Mom said. "Buford Amburgey evicted a family

Afterheat

from his tenant house and they reported him to the health department," she'd warned me. "Had to put in a whole new septic system."

But in the two months my house had sat empty, it had been vandalized twice. Everything left had been loaded up and driven off, someone informed my mother, to Salyersville. The Vance police refuse to reconnoiter Salyersville, where even angels fear to tread.

One Friday night, William calls me. "It's awful pretty down here this time of year," he says. "Now, that's a fact."

"I'm going to hurt you, William, if I don't have that rent in my hand by Wednesday," I tell him.

"Hurt me in a good way?" William says. In the background, I hear a metal banging and the sound of children squealing. "Oh, I think I'd like that. I'll get in my *Impala* and drive up to Massychewsuss for that."

I'm relieved not to have to correct my students: their "I seens," their "Warshingtons," their "we done dids." Without that impossible burden, the locutions have begun to charm me. I never talked much to William as a kid, but I thought about him while I washed dishes or staked tomatoes. I smiled inwardly when I spotted him from my porch swing, admired his fire. I hoped he had the spunk to climb out of the domino life that had been set out for him the day he was born.

William asks me if I'd like him to send a little weed up to Yankeetown.

"Pot just makes me paranoid," I say.

"Well, I myself am having some," William says. I hear a stiff inhale, followed by a contained little cough burst. "No real cash crop left except Mary Wanna."

"You better not be raising pot on my property, William," I say. "I'm dead serious."

"Now, would I do that to you?" William goes on to tell me that pill running and meth cooking is what's really tearing everything up these days. He'd heard that a girl whose parents ran that restaurant downtown got caught up in the pill highway from New York City down to Fort Lauderdale.

"Oh God, William," I say. "It was Wendy, wasn't it?"

"The very girl," William says. "That fellow Devon Weaver turned out to be the mole. Says she ended up at the bottom of a swimming pool breathing through a straw. Well, some kind of tube I guess, cause they weighted her down in the deep end. Knew too much, apparently. Plus, she always had a mouth on

Afterheat
her."

"Did she drown?" I ask, dreading the answer.

"Survived it," William said. "Scared her, though." William goes on to say the ordeal had probably done her good. He heard she got away from the drug runners and revived a little singing career in those music clubs up there.

William calls me every Friday night and sometimes Saturdays. Tonya's got the kids out at Wal-Mart. Tonya is over at her sister's. He is on the front porch having a few beers. If I'm out, I listen to William's messages when I arrive at my studio past midnight—the deep-pitched drawl, his slow cadence and turn of phrase. His voice makes me think of cream pie and the landscape of home, the craggy foothills that shaped him, winged his spirit, and trapped him inside his hardscrabble life. His messages describe his truck breaking down, why the rent is late, why the rent is short. He claims he will Fed-Ex a cashier's check first thing in the morning. I listen to the messages twice, then delete them.

With my teaching experience, it had been easy to find employment in Boston. A kind faculty member at MIT had invited me into her office, and called her contacts around town. In an hour, she'd found me a job teaching English as a second language to scientists on research sabbaticals. My students pay a stupendous amount for my services, and in return, I am paid enough to cover my rent. "Just throw us a bag of peanuts!" my colleagues and I complain when our checks are handed out. Most of them are forced to live at home or in dormitories. I buy groceries from savings accumulated from what I thought were my bottom-dollar years of instruction at Clay County High. As an ESL instructor, I turn out Japanese, European, and South American students who utter scientific terminology in soft Southern accents and tip wait staff in restaurants twenty percent instead of their accustomed five. After three years of applying, I finally received a partial scholarship to the biomedical department at the Sackler School of Medicine. I start classes in the fall.

Deep into the night, I jolt from sleep. An angry sensation snakes up my legs and back, like a wave of chemical fire, weakening me as it passes. My hands tremble, going cold. It's happening, I realize, a cascade of symptoms avalanched through my sleep-slack body. Through the window, Beacon Hill street lamps cast a grainy pink light on my bedclothes. Carefully, I

Afterheat

climb down from the loft bed and close myself behind the French doors of the living room, comforted by floorboards under my bare soles. I pace frenetically back and forth, the way an animal tries to flee its own injury. Breathing slowly, I try to calm myself. The doctors think maybe nightmares trip this neurologic response, but when I wake with a start, dream images are erased.

Panic was of no use. I'd call for help only if I needed the emergency room. Supporting myself on the arm of the couch—I could not keep doing this—I lower myself to my knees. "God help me," said a voice deep in my brain. After the fire, I'd learned to escape my own flesh, fleeing the scalpels and scissors, the chemical scrubs. I hardly felt the determined anesthetist's needles working into my fragile wrists, hardly heard the surgeons complaining about dropping blood pressure or collapsed veins.

The tolling bells at the Park Street church sound hollow and distant. The body is full of irony, seceding from itself to protect itself. Brilliant and foolish, like a virus that reengineers the DNA, then kills its own host. The wave rises again, carrying with it an intolerable pressure, like thumbs gouging my eyes. I was alone, so alone inside my body as I kneel, palms flat, forehead to the smooth, varnished floor.

Sometimes I have to call a taxi to go to the emergency room, or if it's gone too far, an ambulance. The EMT workers hoist my body while it releases the contents of my digestive tract, disgorging even after I've emptied—yellow bile, something resembling coffee grounds, blood-laced saliva—rejecting, without volition, as though I've been poisoned. When I arrive at the emergency room, limp and heaving, unable to talk in whole sentences, blood pressure in my boots, they always suspect drug overdose. "You must sit in this wheelchair, Miss. You must get up."

"IV . . . now," I half shout, grasping for my doctor's letter and my ID. Cascade of symptoms of unknown etiology, the letter explains. Post-traumatic stress disorder, migraine. Please speak softly. Tonight, I am fortunate, and after an hour or so, the waves begin to diminish, each peak a little less than the last, until I am able to turn on my side. I lie still on the floor, thank you God, the bells sounding again, now resonant and warm. I think of Wendy at the bottom of the pool, Wendy singing like a nightingale.

In July, William calls to wish me a happy birthday. "I remember those parties you used to

Afterheat

have," he says. "All those hippies playing Frisbee and badminton on the lawn. All that long hair, Afros, Day-Glo T-shirts, paisley vests." William tells me that he liked to watch me refinishing furniture in the backyard.

"You wore them men's undershirts," he says "Tie-dyed." I hear him sucking in smoke. "No bra," he says holding in smoke. He pauses, exhales luxuriously. "You didn't have curtains on your window."

"I've never liked curtains," I say. "If something is going to get me, I want to see it coming."

I'm glad William isn't here to see blood rising up my neck. This means William would have seen all those hippies spending the night, two to a sleeping bag, caterpillaring around the yard at dawn. He'd seen us working the garden in summer, skinnydipping in the pond, watched me kissing God knows who.

"William, you've got to catch up on your rent," I say, changing the subject, "or you've got to go."

"I know it, I know it," William says. It's an old Kentucky trick, agreeing, to neutralize an argument.

With a steady job, families in Vance can buy a mobile home, or even their own starter house with an FHA loan. So I am stuck with the Williams and Tonyas, Jims and Rosies, the Garnett clan with its missing mother and five recidivist sons. Maybe the farmhouse that I tended for years, devoting every odd moment, every spare dollar, did not represent a step up from a trailer for these folks but a step down. A single-wide trailer anchored on a half-acre lot, at least a family could own that.

On this July night, William is telling me that he pretended to be a dealer and bought a van at the car auction out at the old Sky-Vue Drive-In. It broke down a week later, though, on the way to work. William has a theory that being rich attracts money and being poor is expensive. "They said Oprah Winfrey never pays for her hotel rooms," he says. "Nor a dime for her dinner."

"All those spoiled athletes, too." I say. "I know what you mean."

William, why are you calling me? I want to ask. But that would be too abrupt, too Yankee. The question would embarrass him to the quick. Instead, I lie on my couch half-listening, watching the red bar of sunset melting into the Charles. William speaks more slowly, almost tenderly. There is something he has to tell me, something that's been heavy on his mind.

I sit up on the couch, steadying my body to receive bad news—house burned, mother found dead, dog strangled by fodder twine—my ear pressed hard to the receiver so as not to miss a syllable. "William,

Afterheat
what?"

"My cousins gave me a quarter for every frog."

"You didn't," I say, loosening my grip.

"Yes, ma'am, I did," William admits. "And I'm awful sorry."

"You gigged every last one of my frogs, four for a dollar?" The red sunset out the window turns sinister, blood in the water, oozing down into a tangle of surface waves. I saw them pull a man out of the river once, pale blue, but otherwise perfect, staring up at the sky.

"A quarter, I know," William says, almost whispering. "It seemed like a lot at the time."

Through the hum of the phone wires, I hear a rushing sound, William and I falling away from each other as the answer to my question floats up to me from the magic 8-ball of our ambivalent bond. Why William calls me, why I pick up the phone.

It is not just his urge to confess—a code of ethics in which he can scam rent, steal furniture, raise a crop of cannabis on the sly, yet not be able to lie about frogs. But also, because from his spy place in the pines, he became convinced by the colorful anarchy of my young life, that his life might hold such swaths of what he saw as paradise, if he could only break loose.

And I answer because I want that boy, now man, the dubious custodian of my floors, ceilings, foundations, my temple of stored memories, I want him to tend and protect that secret landscape. I want him to pay, but more than that, I want him to stay. I want him to take care, but why should he? I had to leave, too.

As my house deteriorates, the less rent I will receive, the less I'll be able to repair, the more compromise I'll make in selecting future tenants. William and Tonya are the outlaws who offer the slim protection of fending off other outlaws. For the moment. I am at their mercy, and they won't be sending that rent. It's a socioeconomic truce, cutting a deal with a lick and promise, maximizing the hand they've been dealt.

Soon, I will serve William an eviction notice and pray that I don't have to involve my mother or the police to force the issue in court.

"I hope you like snakes," the Alfreys will call to the new tenants, as they rocket past each other in their overloaded trucks.

I'll welcome the new arrivals, listen to their promises about how they are going to shore up the foundation, repoint the chimney, and paint the rooms

Afterheat
beautiful colors—Persimmon Party, Mexican Coral, Dusky Plum.

Chapter 14
Nightfall

When I answer the phone, I expect my mother, who sometimes calls this time of night but it is my brother, James. "There's no easy way to tell you this." His voice strained high and tight. "Dad's been shot. It was the Stiles girl, Bethel. They've replaced his blood twice already."

"Is he alive?"

"I don't know. They couldn't handle him in Vance, so they sent him over to University Medical Center. They're operating now."

"If I start driving now, I can be there by tomorrow morning. There's no direct flight."

"I don't want you driving," James says. "We can't afford to lose you both in one night."

"Ok," I said. "I'll take a taxi to the airport and

Afterheat
get there as soon as I can."

Seven hours later, I swerve into the hospital entrance and brake the rental car hard behind Mom's illegally parked Lincoln. A silver cigarette lighter lies in the gravel beside the driver's door. When I pick it up, the name Pearl Chambers flashes in the lemony spring sun. A gift from my father, no doubt. He was fond of imprinting the family name all over Creation.

I pass between unpainted concrete columns, through the whoosh of automatic doors into the cool lobby, which smells of star lilies and rubbing alcohol. I move quickly, following the blue line to ICU, a smile from a passing nurse, better than Boston, a real smile. I want to see my father's face, alive, Alive-O.

The number eight lights to my touch and the elevator doors creak close. In the eighth floor lobby, Ray Stacey drops a Styrofoam coffee cup into a swivel-topped wastebasket and hugs me close. The teeth of his motorcycle jacket zipper rasp against my cheek.

"We're still waiting," he says. "They've had him in surgery all night. I'm keeping out of the way. The last thing he needs is to see me."

On tiptoe, I peer through the window of a private room, James' blue Windbreaker hangs over a chairback; a hand, my mother's, taps a cigarette ash into a soda can. She leans forward, saying something, her face obscured by a cloud of smoke, while James nods, his sandy hair shaggy around his shirt collar. I reach for the knob.

"Wait," Ray says. "Before you go in, you ought to know what happened."

I could smell the oil leather of his jacket as he spoke. "They don't know why the girl did it, but evidently she told a fellow waitress down at the Blue Moon that she was planning it. She hasn't been right mentally since her father had his throat slit by her uncle, in a bar fight a couple of years ago.

"How do you know all this?" I ask.

"Horse's mouth," Ray says. "She walked herself downtown, laid the gun on the sheriff's desk and declared, 'I just killed a man up at 417 West Main Street,' like she was talking about the weather. The sheriff went tearing up there, found your dad face down in the yard trying to get to his car. They took one look at him at the Vance ER and knew they weren't equipped for the job. His blood pressure was zero in the ambulance; they've used a dozen pints..."

"Where's Bethel now?" I ask.

"Missing," Ray says. "Wandered off."

Afterheat

I enter the small bright room, leaving Ray in the waiting room. The metal legs of the chair squeaks against the linoleum as my mother rises, envelops me in her aura of tobacco and perfume. "They've got five doctors working on him," Mom says, her voice as dry as kindling.

How to pray in a room full of agnostics, how to join together the three lone souls. James offers a hand to me, the other to our mother, circling the table. Strange to touch his freckled skin, his dense palms and fingers; odd, too, the fragility of my mother's long fingers festooned with rings.

Much later, the head surgeon enters the room. "We're having trouble stopping the bleeding," he says, his voice blunt, though not unkind. The folded down mask reveals a firm, concentrated mouth, his gown dotted with specks of blood. "We're trying one more surgery." He looks at us each directly with dark, intelligent eyes. "But you should prepare yourselves."

When he leaves the room, James begins an incantation, phrases from his Karate katas, "When the enemy comes, circle behind him," his voice wavers, "When he strikes, make yourself water."

I had turned to science; he had turned to martial arts, built a wall of his body. I close my eyes, concentrate—get behind the enemy. Who was the enemy? I wanted to know its face. I'd always thought men were the enemy—holding up vases at auctions, eyes hard as emeralds, hawking the property of the deceased. They chanted ecstatically like Pentecostal healers, "Gimme five, five-fifty, five, who'll go five, going once..." Frankie in his pearl-buttoned shirts. I felt transparent.

James holds my hand firmly. I think of him barefoot in the grass wearing his black karate Gi, hands sweeping, interpreting, twirling faster than I could track with my eyes, mounting the air like a dancer. The three of us hold on, our breaths merged into one breath; walls seem to billow. I picture my father in the operating room, the surgeons quilting him together, membranes, vessels, marrow, and skin.

My mother sleeps on the vinyl couch in the low blue light of the ICU waiting room, while James crouches down in a corner, tamping an unlit cigarette. I descend the bare concrete staircase into the lush Kentucky spring. A bristle-faced farmer in a John Deere cap tucks snuff into his lower lip, while his prodigiously fat wife dispenses bags of potato chips and cans of soda pop to their three children. The wife eyes

Afterheat

me suspiciously, but when I nod in her direction, her face softens to a weary smile, as though acknowledging we are here for the same sad reasons.

The clan looked familiar. The Renfros? The Van Cleeves? Maybe waiting to learn the fates of their sons rolled beneath tractors on steep hillsides, young daughters falling thirty feet from tobacco barn railings onto hard-packed dirt. The children gaze curiously at me as they tear open their chip bags and suck down their sodas. An older sister holds a toddler while he sniffs the bachelor's buttons and Sweet William blooming in the concrete planters. The Stiles clan looks uncannily similar to these folks—wide cheekbones, sharp chins, small, strong, farm-built bodies.

I feel my mother's hand on my shoulder. "You can see your daddy now," she says accepting a light from the farmer.

I turn without answering and rush up the stairs.

"You have one minute," the nurse says, leading me through a maze of doors. "He's extremely tired." A curtain hung from round loops on a suspended rod. The nurse pushes it back.

My father lies under an oxygen tent, his eyes overlarge. An air tube stretches his mouth to a wide impossible O. Bellows frantically pump air into his lungs, breathing for him. Needles, tubes, monitors of all descriptions surround his bed like an army of robots. His skin, shockingly white; his eyes fiery blue. Unable to speak, he bobs his head up and down to me. Straps anchor his arms to the bed, but he raises his right hand, touched forefinger to thumb tip, O-KAY, he signaled me. Going to be okay.

"Let's go, honey," the nurse says, firmly crossing a "t" on his chart and hanging it at the foot of his bed.

Waiting to be buzzed back into the waiting room, I think about my father's underwater training in the army. He told me they'd done simulations in the open ocean, diving seventy feet below the surface, wearing only swim trunks, steel tanks, and goggles. I'd seen newsreels of soldiers jumping off boats, eyes magnified behind masks, hypothermic, surviving on will. Underwater, the soldiers signaled in staccato hand phrases, get with your buddy, low on air, are you A-O-K?

According to my father, the men in his company drank hard, careened down blown-up Japanese roads in Jeeps, knocking over night soil buckets for kicks. In the bathhouses, black-haired girls soaped their backs in exchange for chocolate bars. A raucous bunch, yet

Afterheat

when fathoms underwater, they understood their essential helplessness. I imagined them rising slowly to equalize the pressure in their lungs, breathe in and out, to expel excess nitrogen, flippers gently scissoring the water, slowly, though nearly panicked, wanting to go home to their sweethearts in America—their bombshells, their Pearl Tudors and Angela Jeansonnes. Surfacing in clusters, they tore the oxygen tubes from their mouths and whooped in triumph, bobbing in the water, faces upturned to the sun.

The nurse informs us that there would be no more visits tonight. "Go home," she insists. "Try to rest." Mom and I lean together as we cross the parking lot. I feel as insubstantial as gossamer, my feet barely touching the asphalt. In my mind's eye, my father shrinks smaller and smaller as I move away from the hospital. I never learned to trust that anything would remain as I'd left it. Even though they appear to, people don't get smaller; they don't disappear.

The fragrance of bacon and eggs wake me from a sleep so deep the room around me seems remote, bewildering. Slivers of information glide toward me like filings toward a magnet, in bed, my mother's house, a punching sensation in my solar plexus jackknifed me

in the gold light sifting through the heavy curtains—
my father in intensive care, five bullet holes through
his flesh.

On the sunny kitchen counter, the remains of a
half dozen oranges lie like pop art, a neon apocalypse
of skin cups and tiny tear-shaped fluid sacs, reamed by
the pointed glass juicer. I pour a small glassful. Through
the kitchen screen, a breeze carries the delicate
perfume of the coral bells that grow around the base
beside the gingko tree. A stand of pink columbine nod
like Japanese lanterns, each radiating its own small
sun.

Mom enters the kitchen bearing a few deep
purple tulips, as near as horticulturists could get to
black flowers. "This is the last of them," she says, laying
them on the counter. "Hospital called. Your daddy
made it through the night. They're admitting a miracle.
We can visit at six."

Downtown, Dad's Cadillac is parked in the
drive, recently washed. A few red drops spot the walk
leading into his apartment, but the concrete entryway
had been scrubbed clean. I find the stain in the grass
where the police must have found him.

No police tape cordons off the area, no official
notice taped to the door. Mom had given me the key,

Afterheat

but when I touch the lock, the door swings open. Stepping inside the sunlit room, I find myself face to face with Bethel, carrying an armload of clothes. Clear gray eyes, mesmerizing and cold. When I met her at the farm, she'd seemed like a little girl, but now her face had taken on a timeless quality, mature, unlined. She could have been twenty or forty.

"I'm Claytis' daughter," I say. "Remember?"

Bethel nodded, motioning with her head toward high school portraits of James and me on the wall above the telephone. Bethel finds a paper shopping bag and slides the clothes into it. I was beginning to think she'd become mute, but then she spoke.

"Nobody thought I'd go off like this, not even your daddy, which is, I guess, what saved him. I pointed the gun right at his head. I told him what I was a gonna do. He laughed and told me I was crazy. And I thought, I guess I am, I'm about that crazy. So he goes on over to the TV, turns on *Sixty Minutes*. And I pulled that trigger. When I saw how easy that was, I kept on pulling it. That Mike Wallace got the last bullet."

The dark hulking floor-model television remained on the glass-littered carpet, its tube imploded.

"You should have seen his face, Ruby, like he'd

been clubbed with a thunderstick. And that's just it. I been hit with that attitude like he had all my life, like I couldn't ever do nothin', like I had to just sit there. Nobody ever thought, "Well, Bethel might do something." I told the police that I had killed him, because I thought I had. I didn't mean to kill him. But I did mean to shoot him.

"I heard he was going to make it. That's good for you, Ruby. I know it don't make sense. My daddy was killed, too. It's something I can't think about." Bethel rinses the sponge and squeezes it dry. "Ain't nobody pressed charges. I'm staying at my mom's, out in Rocky Branch. Anybody wants to find me." She pulls off her apron and hooks her purse strap over her shoulder. "I'll leave you be, Ruby. All his things are just like he left them."

Bethel leaves by the front entrance and heads toward town on foot. I stare at the high ceilings and inlaid wooden floors. The furniture is my father's taste—heavy, dark, and functional. Pale squares on the plank floor of the living room showed where a rug has been taken up. The air feels charged, as though still vibrating from the shock of the event that had taken place within its walls. I start toward the bedroom, but freeze with the sudden thought that Bethel might

Afterheat

return. I pause for a long minute, but hear nothing but a family of robins in the tree outside, a mower in the distance, so I step carefully through the threshold.

The bedroom contains an old, carved rosewood bed and matching bureau, and atop the bureau, a glass lion's head I'd given him once for Father's Day. Brave animal, brave man. I believe that you are who you say you are. Inside the top drawer, I find binoculars, bullets, coins, assorted pictures of the Stiles clan, but none of my father and Bethel together.

I couldn't put the two together in my mind, either. I knew she'd shot him, but she seems more like an agent in his destiny than someone to blame. Back outside, I peer down into the grass where he'd lain, my father bleeding out into the long grass. In the ICU, he'd signaled me, making a circle with his thumb and forefinger, going to be O-KAY.

On my way to the hospital that night, I drive past fields of ankle-high wheat, green squares patched with billowing white gauze under which tobacco seeds germinated. I roll down my car window and let the moist, dusky air blow around me. My father had captured his pretty girl, my mother, fathered children, and built a house for us. He worked hard for the life he'd been promised. In the army, he'd learned to follow orders but not to listen. He bought presents, the only kind of love he knew to offer. Give me a beer was all he could think to ask. Give the man a beer or he'll drive you in the ditch till he gets it. Give him the whole damn six-pack.

"Perfect," Dad always claimed, after his yearly physicals—perfect vision, perfect teeth, perfect health. So he had not worn glasses. And when his teeth mysteriously melted, he'd eaten privately because he was ashamed of his dentures. He bet on the horses but threw away his losing tickets, remembering only his victories. He'd worn good dark suits and gold silk ties, his heart closed within him like a mollusk. Finally, my mother divorced him.

A year later, my father knocked on the door of my farmhouse, holding a pail, gloves, seeds, plants, and hoe. We climbed the long hill to the gauze-covered tobacco beds. He pulled up the stakes at one end, worked the ground with his hands and broadcast radish, tomato, red leaf and bib lettuce seeds, pressed soil over the seeds, and repinned the gauze. "In three weeks, we'll make wilted salad," he said, wiping the dirt from his hands with the handkerchief he kept in his pants pocket. I took a good look at him standing

Afterheat

there in the sun, his handkerchiefs, his Brylcreem, his Pepsodent, and his pocket knife, sharpened and oiled.

From my father, I learned to let the weight of the falling blade do its own work of chopping weeds, to plant corn in short rows for better pollination, fuller ears, and to thin carrots by unearthing them by their pungent, lacy tops. I learned to weed in a moist garden, not to walk in a wet one, because it ruined the texture of the soil.

If I couldn't build a house like James, I could at least feed myself. And with that knowledge, I learned to love these hills, the same ones roamed by Iroquois, Shawnee, and Cherokee. The Iroquois had thought of this land as paradise, but they fought too hard to hold on to it, lost too many of their tribe. They'd given up, leaving their dead to its soil, and renamed the state Ka-en-tah-eh, Kentucky, the dark and bloody ground.

A machine stationed near the bed displays two screens: on one, a blue line spikes and falls, noting my father's heartbeats; the bottom screen shows information from his bicep cuff, inflating and deflating at intervals. I hold on to the chilly metal of the raised side rails. My father shifts onto his back and positions his arms to his side. The IV taped to his left arm drips saline into a vein beneath a patch of skin bruised to navy blue. Stretching above the gown's neck, the incisions look taped, too. The blood had been sewn back into its blood sac, not his blood, but James' blood, our mother's blood, the blood of good-willed strangers. My father's heart sucked it in, spurted it out, vessels filled, relaxed, valves within directing the flow.

Two weeks later, I drive to the hospital in the rain. Dad lies on his side, his hospital johnny opened in the back, as James rubs lotion into his shoulders. James had probably never touched our father before, not intentionally.

"Here comes the Yankee," James says as I walk in.

"Straight from Yankeetown." I stand next to him.

It has been two weeks. They'd removed the lung bellows and half the monitors. His face shows color and the hospital gown revealed a suntanned V on his neck and forearms.

James ties the strings of Dad's hospital gown, sits halfway on the bed's edge, his arms crossed over his chest. I pull up a heavy chair.

"Thanks," my father says, his voice hoarse from the tubes.

Afterheat

"I'm going to go smoke one," James says, looking at his watch. "No, I better get on home."

After he leaves, I pick up one of my father's hands, and hold it for a moment. Over the years, the tendons have shortened and stiffened, balling his hands into aching claws so that he can't pick up change from his pockets or lace up his boots.

"What in the world happened, Dad?"

"I don't know what's the matter with that girl," he says. "I tried to help her, get her an education."

I lay his hand back on the bed, wondering if my father talked to Bethel the way he talked to my mother, or to me? Had he ever asked Bethel a question, paid attention to her answer? I slumped under the weight of the terrible, handed-down family silence, my father saluting in family photos, always the stoic, always the soldier. Now, he lies next to me, his body so small and white, like a newborn, his eyes like bits of a sky etched in fire. I wonder, if when he closed them, he remembers looking down the barrel of his own gun, Bethel's gaze falling on him, her deep-down rage.

"Tell me about that envoy you toured with," I say. "You know, with the Emperor."

"Well, our company rode with Hirohito into the countryside," he says, "and at each little town we'd stop, and he'd get out. He was a little fellow, and he'd just stand there silently while we lined up behind him. Then he'd get back in the convoy and drive to the next town. For the first time, the Japanese people heard his voice on the radio, and actually saw him. That's how they knew that he was a man, not a god."

My father looks very tired, his face creased with pain. "We cleaned up over there," he said. "We didn't just leave those people. Fifty years later, they still haven't fought a war."

When he dozes off, I smooth his wavy hair back from his forehead. He is so proud of that hair. I watch him sleep, his chest heaving, crisscrossed with gashes. I pace my own breath with its rise and fall.

I have inherited my father's feral, hermit nature and his taste for stringent food, briny pickles made from baby cucumbers, sandwiches full of mustard, but not his patriotic view of his country where a poor dirt farmer could start his own business, or buy a Cadillac if he wanted one. My father mistook my independence of mind for ingratitude, offended that I couldn't see that every damn thing he'd done was for his family.

After my father drops into sleep, I lay my head on the bed beside him. My father had walked the ruined cities, seen the napalmed land and radiation

Afterheat

sickness with his own eyes. He'd done his duty, then come home to the women who carried the terror for him. Men, blind and weak and violent, believing themselves to be gods.

The next morning, I go jogging on the wet pavement of the subdivision, and the women fly out of their houses in blue and pink jogging suits. I endure their hugs. Yes, he's getting better; I know, it was a shock. These women know me, know to run to me without asking.

Morphine, too much morphine. Too much morphine and he'd gone into a forty-five minute seizure, then a coma, and then shut down. When my father dies, I feel his shoulders superimposed onto mine, widening them. I am driving, but I arrive too late at the hospital. In his room, there is a black rubber sheet over his bed.

"Highly unusual," the nurse says when I insist on seeing him. But she leads me down the stairs, and rolls him out. She unzips the white casing so I can see. His eyes closed, still in his hospital gown, his jaws tied together with a length of sheet. I touch his chest, still warm. The heart, she says, cools last.

CD Collins

The morning of the funeral, thunder cracks the dawn Kentucky sky. Then the sky clears and sun breaks through at the graveside, wind raises the fabric of Father John's black-and-white vestment as though he is about to take wing. Under the green canopy lies my father's pecan wood coffin, draped in the spring flowers brought by Berry Mae. Pots of pink hydrangeas keep blowing over so that my mother and James finally brace them with their feet against the coffin. Afterward, we all sit in Mom's backyard under the mottled sky, Berry Mae, my mother, my brother, and me. We all have the same face now.

Later, as visitors arrive, I drive into town for some takeout barbecue, and then return and park in the driveway. The day I arrived at the hospital, I asked for the clothes my father had been wearing, and was handed a hospital tote. I remember it now, reach behind the driver's seat and pull it onto my lap. I open it and pull out a blood-stained tie, which I slip around my neck.

In the yard next to Mom's, a young boy aims a basketball toward a hoop far too high for his strength. He shoots and shoots, missing every time. It is that dusky moment when the lights of the neighborhood houses appear to illumine all at once. Sitting there,

Afterheat

listening to the tick of the cooling engine and watching the boy, I realized this perception had been an illusion all these years. The lights in the houses do not come on all at once. The effect arises from that one critical degree of nightfall, the contrast with the darkness that makes you notice the light.

Epilogue

I rode in the backseat of the Pontiac, Dad driving, Mom in the front passenger seat. Except for Pa, I resented the men in the family. James with his new train or Dad forgiven for the nights he'd come home drunk or forgotten to come home at all. "He's the boy," my grandmother said, the only explanation ever given for favoring them. But today, looking at Dad in his fedora, the square set of his shoulders, I felt only gratitude. They allowed me to leave the hospital for a few hours, and Dad waited by the entrance for us, the car warmed and ready to go. The backseat of the Pontiac was covered in some kind of plush fabric and the seat felt firm and bouncy.

Dad had told me that my cat, Kilroy, was fine, but I wasn't convinced. People dropped cats off in the country all the time, leaving them to fend for

Afterheat

themselves. If a little animal darted in front of their cars, they didn't even slow down. Dad pulled the car into the gravel drive and switched off the ignition. He buttoned up his overcoat, and then got out and firmly closed the door. Everything he did was measured and precise, like the whole world could wait. The house looked the same as it had the last time I'd seen it, except the trees were stripped down and bare, the wild cherry branches as complicated as dark lace against the late afternoon sky.

The car door suddenly opened and Dad handed me Kilroy, and then got back into the front and smiled at Mom. Kilroy settled onto my lap and purred like an idling diesel. He was a fine gray cat, and though his thick winter coat was cold to the touch, his body was solid and warm beneath. As I stroked him, I felt a softening in my shoulders and my eyes stung with tears. Seeing me, Mom's eyes filled, too. They waited quietly while I held Kilroy, noticing how he purred continuously, inhaling, exhaling, his mouth closed and mysterious. I knew that cats never purred alone.

"We've got to get back," Mom said after a few minutes, "Mrs. Richardson will think we've kidnapped you."

I opened the door, and Kilroy jumped down,

then disappeared across the lawn. Out the window of the Pontiac, the fields rolled out on either side, some rife with red foxtail and purple ironweed, others sown thickly with patches of winter wheat. I thought about how I buried myself in the tall timothy and clover in those fields. The serrated grass blades whipped at my skin and stained my shorts while I daydreamed or brooded. I'd white-knuckled my English racer up steeper and steeper hills, past the Clemmons' horse farm, the Goodpasters' dairy, all the way to the county line. I'd raced home, jumped from my bike, and landed like a panther. I'd been sure of the ground beneath.

CD Collins work includes Blue Land, Self Portrait with Severed Head, Kentucky Stories (winner Best Spoken-Word album Boston Poetry Awards), Subtracting Down, Carousel Lounge, and Clean Coal/Big Lie.

She has been a guest at many venues including Berklee College of Music Performance Hall, John F. Kennedy Center for Performing Arts, Boston's Institute of Contemporary Art and the New York Public Library.

She is currently collaborating on an album of spoken-word with music with Russian-born Santon, a blind, autistic, musical savant and graduate of Berklee College of Music.

more info at www.cdcollins.com

Praise for Blue Land:
"CD Collins has the voice of a natural-born storyteller. Original and Unforgettable."~Stephen McCauley, Novelist
"Altogether brilliant collection..." Ray Olsen, Booklist

Praise for Afterheat:
"With *Afterheat* Collins can lay claim to a serious literary reputation at the level with other contemporary Kentucky writers, such as Bobbie Ann Mason, Barbara Kingsolver, and Silas House."~Kenn Johnson, Journalist

CPSIA information can be obtained
at www.ICGtesting.com
Printed in the USA
FFOW01n2259100116
20225FF